A Candlelight Ecstasy Romance ™

HER WORDS WERE CUT OFF IN A GASP AS HE PULLED HER INTO HIS ARMS. . . .

From the speed of his descent she expected a brutal, ravaging kiss, but his lips were tender and warmly wooing, leading her to respond in spite of herself. And when his lips left hers to travel over her cheeks and eyelids, her mouth blindly sought his for a renewal of that exquisite delight. Then sanity surfaced. She jerked herself out of his arms and over to her own side of the car.

"Come, my little golden witch. Come here, my love." The words were a mere whisper, but they were as effective as a shout. Passion was doused, like a match dropped in water.

She forced amusement into her voice, ignoring its tendency to quaver. "You offer me passion and desire . . . pleasure, but not love. Oh, no, Gareth, I'm not your love."

ALL'S FAIR

Anne N. Reisser

A CANDLELIGHT ECSTASY ROMANCE™

Published by
Dell Publishing Co., Inc.
1 Dag Hammarskjold Plaza
New York, New York 10017

To Bill: he would have been proud

Dell ® TM 681510, Dell Publishing Co., Inc.

Candlelight Ecstasy Romance™ is a trademark of
Dell Publishing Co., Inc., New York, New York.

ISBN: 0-440-10098-4

Printed in the United States of America

First printing—April 1982

Dear Reader:

In response to your continued enthusiasm for Candlelight Ecstasy Romances™, we are increasing the number of new titles from four to six per month.

We are delighted to present sensuous novels set in America, depicting modern American men and women as they confront the provocative problems of modern relationships.

Throughout the history of the Candlelight line, Dell has tried to maintain a high standard of excellence to give you the finest in reading enjoyment. That is and will remain our most ardent ambition.

Anne Gisonny
Editor
Candlelight Romances

"All's fair in love and war."
Francis Edward Smedley

ALL'S FAIR

CHAPTER I

The man was big, powerful, and in a shocking temper. He paced and prowled the waiting room like a sinuous cat recently thwarted of its prey. For the fourth time in as many minutes he stared down at his watch with manifest irritation. Then, having obviously reached the end of his very short patience, he turned toward the apprehensive, though decorative, young woman who regarded him cautiously from behind the long counter that ran along the back wall of the room.

When she had seen him for the first time, an hour ago, she had been immediately impressed by the masculine attractiveness of the tanned, lean-featured face with its startling green eyes and black hair. The high cheekbones and square chin emphasized the strength of the face, and the nose was saved from the effete descriptive "aristocratic" by the obvious fact that it had been broken sometime in the past. The broad-shouldered, lean-hipped body moved with leashed power and athletic grace, lending authority even to the casual Levi's jeans and knitted shirt that molded the powerful muscles of his shoulders and thighs. He carried an expensive but well-worn leather suitcase and an equally expensive briefcase, which he set down

11

just inside the door, dropping the denim jacket he had carried along over his shoulder to rest atop them.

His voice, when he spoke to her as he leaned casually on the counter, was a deep, rich baritone and sent delightful shivers down her spine. His words, however, chased cold chills back *up* her spine.

"I'm Gareth Hammond," he announced politely. "I've chartered one of your planes to fly me into Buckeye. Will you notify the pilot that I'm here and ready to go? I'm already running behind schedule, and I'd like to take off as soon as possible."

She gulped, inaudibly, she hoped. *Oh glory! He would be the one!* She moistened the lower lip of her rather full, reddened mouth and smiled confidingly up at him.

"Well, actually, Mr. Hammond, there's . . . uh . . . been a slight problem. We . . . I tried to reach you at your hotel, but you'd already left. The pilot who was scheduled to fly you up there, well, his wife went into the hospital to have a baby and he went with her. It's their first and they're doing it with natural childbirth and he . . ." Her voice faltered into silence beneath the impact of the gaze that had suddenly gone as cold as the heart of an iceberg.

"My dear young woman." His stern voice indicated that she was anything but. "Am I to understand that there is no pilot available to honor the charter arrangements? I was told that your company was the most reliable and efficient in this area, which"—he paused ominously—"is why I directed my firm to draw up *tentative* contracts with your company to handle the supply and personnel transfers that setting up the Buckeye operation will entail."

The inflection on the "tentative" did not escape her notice, and she rushed into further speech.

12

"Oh, no, sir, Mr. Hammond. We have another pilot. It's not that! It's just that when the new pilot went to preflight the airplane, it was discovered that there was something wrong with the engine. It's being repaired right now. There'll only be a very slight delay"—she crossed her fingers behind her back—"and you'll be on your way. I just tried to let you know at your hotel so that you wouldn't rush out here."

That had been an hour ago. For the first half hour he had worked silently on papers that he withdrew from the briefcase and spread over the battered wooden table that, with the three folding chairs and rather lumpy couch, constituted the rest of the "waiting" area of the room. Behind the counter she made a pretense of filing, afraid to type the letters awaiting transcription lest the noise act as an added irritant.

At the end of the first half hour he had shoved the papers back into the briefcase and begun to prowl restlessly. He refused her offers of coffee with sardonic politeness, and his glances at his watch came more and more frequently. Now he was striding toward the counter, and she reluctantly moved forward to meet him.

"Yes, Mr. Hammond? I'm *so* sorry for the delay. I'm sure it will only be a little longer." She smiled again, using her highest voltage smile, and raised long eyelashes in a practiced gesture. Both smile and gesture bounced off and lay frozen to death, executed by the cold fury in his green eyes.

"Which hangar is the plane in? I'll talk to the mechanic myself," he announced grimly.

She was only too willing to give him directions. "Go out the front door and turn left. It's the middle hangar, and the plane is the red Cessna." She watched him wheel and stride to the door, impatience in every long step. She was overdue for a coffee break, and she rather thought a cup of hemlock might taste delicious right now!

With a jaw that jutted pugnaciously, Gareth followed the directions and strode through the bright afternoon sunlight toward the middle of the three hangars. When he entered the center hangar, he paused for a moment to let his eyes adjust to the cooler dimness.

Before him crouched the recalcitrant plane, engine cowling raised. The shapeless figure of an overall-draped mechanic worked with seeming industry on the innards of the plane, accompanied by a low, tuneless, hissing whistle that echoed faintly in the high-ceilinged building. Gareth stood silently for a moment, observing, but the figure of the mechanic showed no awareness of his presence.

"How much longer will it take to get this crate into airworthy condition?" he finally rasped out.

The stooped figure straightened abruptly, with unfortunate, but totally predictable, results. A knitted cap, pulled low to the ears, cushioned the blow somewhat, but there was still a satisfying, ringing *thunk* when the top of the mechanic's head met the underside of the raised cowling. A muffled but none the less explicit epithet sizzled in the air, and the figure swung with cautious but undeniable grace to face the scowling man.

The mechanic, encased in heavily grease-smeared, exceedingly baggy coveralls raised two arresting, turquoise-blue eyes in an unloving, encompassing glance that traveled up from Gareth's toes to settle with piercing precision on his wrathful face. The turquoise eyes, glaring from a smudged, grease-streaked face, turned icily chill, and a voice to match dripped icicles as it said. "It'll take another five minutes to be sure she'll get off the ground. If you

14

want assurance that she'll come down again in one piece, that'll be fifteen minutes longer."

The figure then returned its attention to the intestines of the balky engine and resumed work. Gareth stood in silent, somehow menacing, immobility for the stated time. At almost to the second the cowling was lowered and latched into place.

After wiping very greasy hands on a piece of rag, the mechanic carried the tools over to a metal box, sorted and stowed them, and then closed the lid with a reverberating clang, snapping a padlock through the hasp. As a hand swept up to pull off the cap, Gareth was heard to mutter, "A damned woman mechanic."

Once again turquoise eyes raked him, then the hand completed the tugging motion. Hair like molten honey spilled from the confining cap and tumbled past stiffly held shoulders.

"It's a damned woman *pilot* too, Mr."—the faintest pause and lifting of an arched slim brown eyebrow— "Hammond. If you will get your bags while I clean my hands and get out of this coverall, we'll be on our way."

She started to turn away, pulling at the zipper of the coverall to reveal a tanned throat and the collar of a faded flannel shirt.

"Just a minute, young woman!" Gareth barked sharply. "Do you work for this company? There was no mention of a woman pilot when we investigated the company prior to awarding the contract. I understood that there were three male pilots, including the owner."

"Your investigations were accurate, Mr. Hammond," she assured him evenly. "There are three *male*"—she mimicked his slight stress of the word—"pilots, two of whom are on other assignments. The third pilot is by his wife's

15

side as she undergoes the birth of their first child. I do not work for the company, but the third pilot is my brother. When he had to take his wife to the hospital, he called me and asked if I would fill in for him. I agreed to do so."

She turned away again, walked over to a wall of the hangar, finished wriggling out of the coverall, and draped it over a nail protruding from the wall. She then washed her hands and face at a nearby sink and dried them on the rough white towel that dangled from another large nail. When she turned to go back to the plane, she discovered that he was still standing exactly where she'd left him.

His eyes raked over her, taking in the free-flowing hair, the faded shirt, sleeves rolled up above her elbows, and the equally faded shorts that left her long, golden-tan legs bare until they disappeared into sockless tennis shoes. Her lips tightened slightly, but the look she gave him expressed only calm inquiry.

"Is there anything else, Mr. Hammond? I understood that you were eager to get to Buckeye. It's an hour's flying time up there and an hour back for me. Sunset is in three hours. This plane is equipped for instrument flying; however, I prefer not to have to bring it back late tonight."

"Yes, there is *something* else, young woman," he began.

"My name is Morgain Kendrick, Mr. Hammond. You may call me Miss Kendrick," she interrupted coldly. "I prefer it to 'young woman.'"

His green eyes flared black for a fleeting second, and a small muscle bulged at the corner of his jaw. The air crackled with an aura of thinly suppressed violence, and the clash of wills was as audible as the sound of steel on steel in a saber duel.

"Very well, *Miss Kendrick*. To continue, your brother is presumably a competent pilot. That fact does not, how-

16

ever, have any bearing on *your* qualifications as a *pilot.*"
The faint stresses on the words, accompanied by an encompassing glance that appreciated the slender waist and high, firm young breasts brought a hard, angry flush to her cheekbones. He continued in the same mocking, deep voice, "I do not propose to entrust myself to the tender mercies of someone who was given lessons by big brother and has managed, somehow, to acquire a private pilot's license plus a hundred hours of flight time. I am sure you have many talents, Miss Kendrick, but I am not at present in need of any of them."

With a truly heroic effort Morgain kept her voice perfectly level. "Mr. Hammond, the only one of my *talents* available to you, now or ever, is that of pilot. For your information"—each separate word was carved in ice—"I taught my brother how to fly. I've been flying since I was fourteen. I have over three thousand hours of flight time and I hold a commercial pilot's license, multiengine jet. I am a second officer on a B-727. I am employed in that capacity by Trans-Countries Airlines."

She paused for breath and continued in the same level tone, "I started a month's vacation yesterday and came home to spend it with my parents, which is why I was available to help my brother when he called. Now, Mr. Hammond, *if* you have no further questions concerning my qualifications, the plane will be available for takeoff for the next five minutes. After that I will assume you wish to make other arrangements, which you are more than welcome to do. The *male* pilots who work for this company will be available to fly you wherever you wish to go tomorrow." Each inflection of that icily level tone indicated just *where* she thought a suitable destination should be.

17

"In six minutes I will leave and resume my interrupted vacation."

There was absolute silence, except for the soft pad of her tennis shoes as she walked with swift, lithe strides to the plane, opened the door on the pilot's side, and climbed in. The click of the latch when she secured the door was very soft and *very* final.

Morgain stared at John with dismay. He had contacted her at her parents' home on the second morning after she had flown Gareth Hammond up to Buckeye and had asked her to come down to his office. She had gone readily. He deserved to hear a full, first-person account, and to be forewarned, about the contretemps between herself and one of his biggest potential clients. Of course, she wasn't actually an employee of John's, so he couldn't really be blamed for her lapse into bad manners, or shouldn't be blamed, she amended mentally, but that overbearing, arrogant, totally infuriating man would probably be petty enough to take it out on poor John. . . .

She had jerked her attention back to the big, balding man whose warm, worried brown eyes were regarding her so hopefully.

"I know it's a lot of cheek to ask you to give up most of your vacation and work, Morgain love, but I'm really in a cleft stick. Of all the fool things for Jerry to do . . . to trip over a bar of soap and break a leg in the shower! We've got to start hauling stuff to Buckeye the day after tomorrow, and that puts us one man behind the eight ball. I can't let my other obligations slide, but I'm under contract to Hammond Enterprises now and I must honor their requirements first."

"But John, I don't understand!" What an understatement! "When did you sign the final contract? I thought Gareth Hammond was still up at Buckeye. He wasn't due back until the end of the week. And Jerry broke his leg yesterday so you knew . . ." Morgain's thoughts were whirling frantically.

"Hammond radioed for a pickup yesterday afternoon and we signed the contract this morning. I told him about Jerry yesterday, when I flew up and got him, but I told him that I'd try to get a replacement pilot to cover for Jerry until he's out of the cast. Hammond suggested you. You must have made a good impression on him the day you ferried him up there."

Her mouth fell open in astonishment. "B...b...but that's crazy! John, look, there's something you obviously don't know. I had one hell of a run-in with Mr. Gareth Hammond the day I took Ken's place, while Jenny was having the baby."

Morgain described the happenings in graphic detail and concluded, ". . . and the entire flight was made in complete and chilly silence. He worked on papers from his briefcase, and I flew the plane. The stop on the strip at Buckeye was the nearest thing you can get to a touch-and-go landing and still discharge a passenger. He got out of the plane, hooked his suitcase out of the back, shut the door, and I was rolling. He *can't* have recommended me for anything but slow and exquisite torture or possibly boiling in oil."

She drew in a deep breath and expelled it in a long sigh. "No. I'm sorry, John." She didn't *sound* sorry. "It's out of the question. There must be some other way." *And you'd better find it fast,* Morgain's stormy face implied.

Gareth Hammond had *not* made a good first impression on Morgain. She had no desire to give him a chance to make a worse one the second time. There wasn't going to *be* a second time!

"Morgain, believe me," John responded heavily. "I've thought and thought. Where could I get some competent pilot by tomorrow, and for just six weeks? You know that there's no one local available who can fly under the conditions we'll be encountering. All I need is a breathing space. Give me three weeks and I'll be able to shift some of our other commitments and arrange schedules so that Ken and I can carry Buckeye, and whatever else I can't put off, until that fool Jerry gets his cast cut off. Morgain," he hesitated and then continued, "I have to have the Buckeye contract. We went through a bad patch a year ago and I almost lost the business. The Buckeye contract will pull us through and start us on the upward road again."

She was fighting a losing battle and she knew it, but she had to give it one more shot. "Look, John," she reminded him, "if I fly for you as an employee, you'll be responsible for my behavior. Now Gareth Hammond and I just do not, and will never, get along. The man has a natural propensity for setting my back up, and believe me, it's mutual. You should have seen the way he looked at me the first time we met . . . the only time we'll meet if I'm lucky." She smiled her most winning smile. John was not visibly won.

Gamely she continued, "If I'm flying for you, we're bound to come into contact now and again, and with the best will in the world, I can't promise to be polite to him if he starts using that sarcastic, sneering tongue on me." She gave a rueful grin. "Grandfather Ryan may not have bequeathed his red hair to me like he did to Ken, but he certainly passed down his temper . . . 'the devil's own,' as my father says."

John's hearty laugh boomed out in the cluttered office. "Truer words were never spoken, Morgain, as I can attest, having been on the receiving end of your temper a time or two myself! You are really deceptive packaging, my love. A face like a sleepy angel . . . with that hair and those blue eyes . . . you should be forced to wear a sign: 'Warning! Concealed Redhead! Irritate at your own risk.' "

He sobered again. "I'll make a deal with you. I'll do my best to keep you out of Hammond's way if you'll give me those three weeks. You can fulfill all of those other commitments for me and Ken or I will do the Buckeye loads. Fair enough?" He spread his large hands appealingly.

What could she say? "All right, John," she acquiesced glumly, with grave reservations and misgivings. "I only hope we don't all live to regret this. When do you want me to start? And it can't be today because I have a date this afternoon and evening."

"Tomorrow will be fine," he sighed in relief. He could afford to quit . . . he was ahead. "There are three consignments that have to go out, all in three different directions. Seven o'clock show time, I'm afraid, so I hope you weren't planning a long evening out."

"Nope, just dinner and a little dancing, I think, and this afternoon I'm just going along for the ride." She rose and threw a two-fingered salute to her temporary boss. "See you tomorrow, slave driver."

After lunch Morgain and her mother stood in well-practiced harmony, dealing with the luncheon dishes. The gentle sapphire eyes, so like yet unlike her own, gazed worriedly at her.

"But, Morgain, dear, this is your vacation. You came home to rest, and besides, after what you told us about

21

your encounter with Mr. Hammond, I should think John would want to keep you two as far apart as possible."

Morgain grinned, a nonladylike lifting of finely molded lips. "John is what is popularly known as 'between a rock and a hard place'! He has to have the contract from Hammond and he has to honor his other commitments. Jerry was so unobliging as to have his accident *now*. . . ." She shrugged and continued, "Mom, you know I owe John a lot. He taught me to fly, let me mess around the planes as much as I wanted to, and encouraged me to try for the job with T.C., which I love. There is another aspect as well." She shot her mother a teasing glance. "There's Ken. His job depends on the health of John's business. With the expenses of the new baby he and Jenny don't need the worry of finding a new job and relocating. I don't want you and Dad to miss your chance to be doting grandparents . . . ah ha! . . . I see that aspect didn't occur to you." Morgain chuckled at her mother's horrified expression.

She wrinkled her patrician nose and bewailed, "I knew it! You'd throw your only daughter to the wolves . . . or a wolf in business man's clothing . . . without a qualm for the sake of your new grandbaby. Admit it!"

Her mother considered the accusation judicially for a moment . . . only a moment . . . and then responded, "Well, I think that's overstating the case somewhat. I'd have *a* qualm. After all, you are my only daughter, as you've just reminded me. But then, Jeremy *is* my only grandchild!"

Morgain flicked a glob of soapsuds at her laughing parent and then dodged agilely away as her mother snapped a dish towel at her long, bare legs. While the water gurgled out of the sink, she dried and inspected her long-fingered, graceful hands and shook her head. "Tch, tch." She clicked her tongue in mock dismay. "A terminal case of dishpan hands if ever I saw one. Hand me the lotion, nurse, and we may save them yet."

"If you'd wear these rubber gloves I procured for you at such great expense . . ." her mother began in the honeyed tone of one who has said the same words many times.

"Hands heal, dishes don't," retorted her daughter briskly, "If you will recall, the last time I wore a pair of rubber gloves to wash dishes, I broke two cups and chipped a plate. The pesky things get in my way and they feel *yucky.*"

"Yucky!" Her mother rolled her eyes at the inelegant term and then returned to the previous subject. "Well, since you're determined to stick your head into the lion's mouth . . . I just hope John has his insurance up to date and his antacid tablets close to hand." She abandoned that topic as a lost cause. "By the way, will you be home for dinner tonight?"

"No, Tige Anderson is coming by for me in an hour. We're going over to Grenville for the afternoon and then he's taking me to dinner at the hotel tonight. It won't be a late night, though, since I have an eight-o'clock flight time tomorrow, which means a seven o'clock show time."

"I expect we'll see a lot of Tige now that you're home," her mother commented with limpid innocence. "He called me three times the day you were due in, asking if you'd arrived yet."

Morgain accepted the thrust and parried. "I know. He told me. Did I tell you that he's been to see me twice in San Francisco? He was in town on business for Hammond Enterprises and I happened to be between flights each time, so we went out for dinner and to the theater."

Morgain finished rubbing the lotion into her hands and proceeded to squash firmly her mother's matchmaking propensities. "He's very nice and I enjoy going out with him, but that is *all,* so remove that hopeful-mama gleam from your eyes, my esteemed parent! I've enjoyed going out with other men, too, and I have no desire to settle on any particular one at my tender age," she continued dryly. "I'm sure, in due time, I will present you with the most marvelous son-in-law you could ever desire, but not now. I have a job I love, opportunities to travel . . . why should I give all of that up for a husband?"

She didn't wait for an answer to her rhetorical question. A wicked gleam sparkled in her blue eyes as she assumed a deeply thoughtful expression and tapped one long forefinger against her pursed lips. "I'll tell you what I will do, though. I know you have high standards where a prospective son-in-law is concerned, so why don't we draw up a spec list? I'll check all candidates against your requirements so that when the time comes and I'm ready to settle down, I won't have to waste time weeding out undesirables. Let's see. He'll have to be intelligent, thoughtful, and kind. Do you prefer tall, dark, and handsome or tall, fair, and handsome? I'll do my best to fulfill any reasonable request," Morgain promised obligingly and outrageously.

Her mother's chuckle echoed her own. "At the top of my list would be the requirement that he be big enough and determined enough to turn you over his knee whenever you needed it!" was her mother's spirited retort. "How two such mild people as your father and I ever came to have such a willful daughter I'll never know."

"Huh, blame it all on Grandfather Ryan. You always do." Morgain's voice dropped an octave and took on the rumbling vowels of her father's slow speech. " 'She's pure Ryan, Miri my love. I've seen that scowl on your father's face a hundred times before.' And that's a direct quote, as I'm sure you recognize. Daddy must have said *that* a hundred times, and rank slander it is! I never scowl! It isn't ladylike, and besides, it encourages wrinkles." She simpered sickeningly.

By this time mother and daughter were laughing so hard that it was impossible to continue. They exited from the kitchen, arms about each other's waists, heads of honey gold and silver-frosted red close together. They separated in the hall, Morgain to change for her afternoon with Tige, and Miri to make yet another visit to her new grandson and daughter-in-law.

As they drove along the winding back road Tige glanced over at Morgain where she sat, half turned toward him, humming under her breath in happy accompaniment to a song that was playing softly on the car radio.

"You look extraordinarily cheerful this afternoon. Any particular reason, or may I hope it's merely the pleasure of my company?" he asked lightly.

"It must be the pleasure of your company," she answered with a wry smile. "I have a feeling that the next three weeks are going to be a bit hectic. Certainly they won't be the restful vacation I had in mind." Her eyes considered the passing scenery with an unseeing stare.

"What do you mean? Has something gone wrong at home?" He voiced his concern instantly, and glanced again at her with a troubled expression. "Is there anything I can do to help?"

"Thanks, Tige, you're very sweet, but no, there's nothing you can do, and everything is fine at home. The crisis is all due to a bar of soap, and really, it won't be too bad. In fact, it will give me a chance to repay some of a long-standing debt." She laughed at his frankly puzzled expression and began to explain.

"It's just that this has suddenly turned into a working vacation for me. You see, Jerry McMichaels, John's other pilot, slipped in the shower and broke his leg, leaving John a pilot short, with no replacement available. The Buckeye shipments start day after tomorrow, and John needs three pilots so that he can fulfill all of his commitments. I've promised to help him out for the three weeks I'm here, starting tomorrow."

"But you shouldn't have to give up your vacation. I know how you were looking forward to it." His protest was immediate and sympathetic, and he was conscious of personal disappointment when he realized that her free time would be markedly curtailed if she had to start flying charters. "Do you really have to do it?"

"Well, yes, I do. You see, John taught me how to fly and he's been a very good friend to me." She debated whether to forgo all mention of Mr. Gareth Hammond. The less said and seen of him, the better, as far as she was concerned. "Actually, I'm glad of the chance to help John out. There were other factors involved that made me less than enthusiastic when John first asked for my help, but he promised to do his best to help me avoid certain . . . ah . . . problems I foresaw arising. Anyway, it's only for three weeks and 'needs must when the devil drives.' "

She began to talk of other things, and he followed her lead with resigned amiability. When Morgain changed the subject so relentlessly, he knew it was useless to pursue it further. When they reached the surveyor's office in Gren-

26

ville, he guided the car into a convenient parking slot and smiled at Morgain.

"What will you do while I'm seeing Poston? It'll take me an hour, and it's too hot for you to wait in the car."

"I have a few errands and an old friend I promised to stop by to see, so I'll keep occupied," she assured him. "Shall I meet you out in front in about an hour?"

"That's fine," he agreed readily. "If I'm going to be longer, I'll come out and tell you." He watched her walk away with a free, swinging stride, and noted that his was not the only appreciative masculine eye to follow her progress down the street. She walked with high-headed pride and a collected grace that was a pleasure to observe. Her bright hair glittered in the sun, seeming to trap the warm rays in its silken net. When she turned the corner, moving out of his sight, he left the side of the car and entered the office building for his conference.

Right on time, an hour later, Tige and Gareth Hammond completed their consultation with the surveyor and paused in the spacious anteroom of the office to confirm details of the work schedule for the following week.

"Excuse me a moment, Gareth," Tige interrupted, "I want to see if Morgain's waiting outside for me. I told her I'd be done about now, and she said she'd meet me at the car."

Tige crossed to the bay window overlooking the street, and to his surprise Gareth followed him, to stand beside him while they scanned the street.

They were just in time, because they saw Morgain making her way back toward the car. She was dressed in hip-riding jeans and a striped cotton sun top that bared a tanned, taut midriff. Her feet were in tennis shoes again, without the benefit of socks, and the shoes' tongues were

27

tied outside the uppers by the laces, which were only threaded through the lowermost holes. Her hair was pulled into a cascading ponytail atop her head for coolness, and if one could ignore the eyecatching figure displayed by the covering (but not detracting) clothes, one might have imagined her to be a child ready for a day's fishing, complete with cane pole and a can of worms, under some cool willow-overhung stream bank.

She leaned comfortably back on the fender of Tige's car, propped one foot on the bumper, and rested a forearm along the thigh of the raised leg. The other arm and hand were busy conveying a two-scoop ice-cream cone to her waiting mouth, where her tongue efficiently dealt with the inevitable rivulets of melting ice cream.

The watching men observed her unself-conscious absorption in the ice cream while she savored it with the enthralled, singleminded passion of the very young.

Tige sighed. "Three weeks ago I took her to dinner at the Top of the Mark in San Francisco. She had on a slinky green thing." He gestured expressively. "It had every man in the place ready to knife me in the back. Today she looks thirteen years old."

Gareth lifted a mocking eyebrow. "Hardly thirteen, I would say, but I see your point. A woman of many facets. Quite a challenge." His voice was musing and his gaze speculative.

Tige looked at him uneasily. Gareth had a reputation for enjoying the company of beautiful women, and an equal reputation for extricating himself smoothly whenever there was the slightest hint of possessiveness or desire for a closer relationship on the part of these women. One of the discarded beauties, bitter and resentful, had likened him to a panther who enjoyed the hunt but walked away

28

free while his prey lay bleeding on the ground. Even allowing for spite and exaggeration, Tige felt that there might be more than a grain of truth in the word picture conveyed by those bitter gibes. From the thick black hair and powerful shoulders, down the long muscular legs, there was power and arrogance radiating from every inch of the man next to him. Tige knew from firsthand observation that Gareth could display a ruthless sense of purpose in his business dealings, and it required no imagination to believe that it could be the same in his dealings with women.

"Do you see much of . . . ah . . . Morgain?" Gareth's deep voice jerked Tige from his introspection.

"As much as she'll let me. She is domiciled in San Francisco and only visits her parents occasionally."

"So that's why you've been so eager to volunteer for the trips to San Francisco recently" was Gareth's dry rejoinder. "I thought it was merely an admirable devotion to duty. Instead of burning with ambition, you were burning with desire." The drawling tones brought a flush to Tige's fair skin, and he turned quickly to his employer and friend.

"Now, listen to me, Gareth," he snapped. "I know you don't have a very high opinion of women in general, but Morgain's different. She's not a girl for a casual affair, and she's no grasping, brainless beauty either."

He would have continued in the same heated vein, but a sudden thought struck him. Morgain had a distinct aversion to predatory males. She saw too many of them among her working companions, and she had often commented on her opinion of men who saw women as little more than bedmates and entertainment for a short term. She was no rabid enthusiast of women's liberation, preferring to be what she called a person liberationist, where

29

everyone was accepted for himself or herself, regardless of sex, according to their abilities and personalities. If Gareth Hammond decided Morgain was quarry he was interested in hunting, Tige would put his money on Morgain any time!

He changed his earlier plan, to avoid an introduction between Gareth and Morgain if at all possible, and instead said, "Come on out and meet her, Gareth. We're done here and I want to run Morgain home so that she'll have plenty of time to get ready for our dinner together tonight." Unholy mischief glinted in his eyes.

As he spoke he drew the taller man along with him toward the door. The opened front door let in a blast of heat that swept aside the air-conditioned coolness of the office. While the two men descended the shallow steps to the sidewalk, Morgain popped the last bite of the cone into her mouth and balled the napkin up in her hand. She looked up and saw the men coming toward her. Her expression froze momentarily. Tige saw an icy glaze skim over her eyes before her lashes swept down for a moment, shielding her gaze. When she lifted her lids again, her expression was inscrutable, but he fancied there was a wary tenseness about the set of her shoulders as she watched them approach.

She pushed away from the car's fender and smiled warmly up at Tige. "All done, Tige?" She turned her head slightly and her smile faded. "Good afternoon, Mr. Hammond." Her voice was pleasant but neutral, and Tige gaped at her slightly.

"Do you know each other?"

"We've met" was her unrevealing reply.

"Miss Kendrick flew me to Buckeye several days ago," was Gareth's little-more-revealing contribution.

"Oh." Tige could think of nothing else to relieve the bald inadequacy of the single word.

There was a brief, charged silence, and though Tige shifted restlessly, Morgain and Gareth stood relaxed and balanced, neither showing embarrassment or recognition of the crackling tension in the air.

"I understand that you're going to be working for us for three weeks, Miss Kendrick. It's very good of you to give up your vacation to help us out after Mr. McMichaels' unfortunate accident." Gareth's smooth tone reflected only courteous interest.

Morgain stiffened infinitesimally, but her voice was just as courteous and smooth when she replied. "I'm always glad to be able to help out a friend, but I'm afraid you're laboring under a misconception, Mr. Hammond. I'll be working for John, not Hammond Enterprises, and since I will be fulfilling John's other commitments, I shan't have any contact with the Buckeye consignments."

Her smile this time was filled with genuine amusement. "John or Ken will take care of the Buckeye flights to your complete satisfaction, I'm sure." She linked arms with Tige and cocked her head at him. "Are you ready to go, Tige? I'll wait in the car if you have something further to discuss with Mr. Hammond." As she released his arm she nodded at Gareth and bade him a polite farewell, leaving the men to make their own farewells.

Morgain slid into the hot interior of the car, wincing slightly as the bare skin of her back momentarily contacted the hot upholstery. She made haste to roll down the windows of the car, the small job allowing her to ignore the presence of the two men still standing by the car's front bumper. The glare from the windshield protected her from their sight, she knew, and she was grateful, be-

31

cause the flush that had risen to her cheeks was not due to the heat of the day.

"It's very good of you to give up your vacation to help *us* out . . ." Her mind accurately played back each word he had uttered in that dark, deep baritone. To anyone listening it was merely smooth courtesy, but to Morgain's ear the undertone of mockery came through clearly and distinctly. John had better hold to his word to keep her off the Buckeye runs or there would be murder done yet. All of her previous misgivings came back a hundredfold, and she wished with prescient intensity that John had not prevailed upon her to take on this job.

Tige opened his door and slid into the driver's seat. She concentrated on buckling her seat belt, glad not to meet his glance for the moment, until she was sure she had mastered her expression. He buckled his own seat belt. Neither spoke while he reversed the car out of the parking slot and onto the street. As they drove out of town he seemed to be nerving himself to open a subject that might be touchy, and the sidelong glances he kept casting toward her were a measure of his disquiet.

"Um, Morgain. Was it my imagination, or was there just the slightest bit of tension between you and Gareth? I know you've a perfect right to tell me it's none of my business, but . . ."

"It's all right, Tige. I don't mind your knowing, and you did catch the fringes of the backlash." Once again she briefly related the bare details of the encounter, and Tige's low whistle when she concluded was comment enough. "I promised to help John out, but only on condition that he or Ken handle Buckeye. You can see that if Mr. Hammond and I come into contact too often, there's liable to be an allmighty conflagration. I know my own weaknesses, and placid temperament is not one of the blessings my good fairies handed out to me at my birth. For myself, I don't care, but as long as I'm John's employee he's in some measure answerable for my shortcomings. I'm perfectly willing to carry on a running battle with Mr. Hammond if he forces the encounters, but I don't want John being shot down as an innocent bystander." Her husky chuckle was rueful. "I'll do my best to avoid open hostilities, and as long as Mr. Hammond and I don't come into contact too frequently, or for too long a span at any one time, perhaps we'll squeak through these three weeks without major confrontations. Can I count on you to help me avoid your boss whenever possible?"

"Lord, yes, Morgain. I had no idea all this was going on. I'll do whatever I can to help." He grinned. "I'll be happy to keep you as far away from Gareth as I can manage."

She laughed delightedly. "Beautifully put."

"I thought so myself," he averred modestly. "And in earnest of my promise, may I take you out to dinner tomorrow night, too?"

"I'd enjoy that very much, Tige, subject to what John has lined up for me the day after, but I didn't mean that I needed to be kept away from him socially. I'm not in any danger from him that way. I'm not his type."

"Beautiful women are his type, Morgain dear, and that very definitely makes *you* his type."

She laid a finger on the point of her chin and simpered at him. "A most graceful compliment. Thank you, kind sir. Perhaps I should rephrase that. He's not *my* type. I may be forced to associate with him in business situations, but I still retain control over my social life." Her lips tightened, and a militant gleam sparkled in her eyes. "I

33

think I'm capable of holding my own against Mr. Hammond in a social situation, in the unlikely event that one should arise. But please, let's find a more congenial topic of conversation for the ride home. I've always thought that there was good sense in the 'out of sight, out of mind' platitude."

Tige was only too ready to agree, and the rest of the ride passed in happy harmony, enlivened by Morgain's wickedly humorous vignettes of some of her experiences on recent trips, especially those on the route called the desert patrol, which plied the air lanes between Los Angeles and Las Vegas and back again.

"You wouldn't believe some of the outfits we see on those runs," she chuckled wickedly as they drew up in front of her parents' house. "Why, I heard of one captain who was nearly crushed to death by the first officer and the second officer when all three tried to get a look at one lady who was boarding the plane. The captain sits in the left seat in the cockpit, you see, and the passengers board from that side too. Well, it seems that the captain made a comment on the lady's . . . ahem . . . well-displayed attributes and was trapped in the rush to enjoy the view from his window. Fortunately, I suppose, the window was closed at the time or he would probably have been squeezed out of it like toothpaste out of a tube, but I do understand that his nose will never be the same again. The airline turned down his request for compensation, though he did claim it was a job-related injury. . . ."

Tige was laughing so hard that he could barely negotiate the driveway, and after he had wiped the tears from the corner of his eyes, he shook his head in remonstrance. "Don't ever tell that story to anyone driving on a freeway. You'll cause the most awful pileup. . . ."

"Thanks for the ride, Tige. You do know that it'll have to be an early night tonight? I've got a seven o'clock show time tomorrow morning, and I really need to be there a bit earlier to bring my local maps up to date." She forestalled him as he started to get out to come around and open her door. "No, don't get out. You have to get on to the office and I'm going to run next door to see MaryAnn for a moment. What time tonight?"

"Hmm," he considered. "Since you're a working girl again I'll pick you up at six. Not much time for wining, dining, and dancing if we leave much later than that."

"You may dine and dance with me, but not wine me, I'm afraid," she demurred ruefully. "I'm strictly teetotal the night before a flight. Alcohol and airplanes don't mix at all well in my opinion. Put the Château Lafite back in the refrigerator and we'll save it for the end of my vacation, such as it is."

She slid out of the car and shut the car door gently. She gave him a gay wave as he pulled out of the driveway, but her face assumed grim lines as soon as he was out of sight. It was all very well to pretend insouciance in front of Tige, but she was deeply disturbed. She started toward the next-door neighbor's house, but changed her mind. MaryAnn would keep.

Morgain went around in back of her parents' home and made her way to the peeling garden swing beneath the welcome shade of the gnarled apple tree that had sheltered her in her childhood and had contributed the wherewithal for many a green-apple stomachache to the neighborhood children. She plumped several faded cushions into a back-rest against the arm of the swing, and stretched out full length, dangling one long leg down to push the swing into motion with the tip of her toe. The rhythmic creak of the

35

chains should have been soothing, but she found that the familiar sounds and rhythms were no panacea for her troubled thoughts.

She considered what she knew, and feared, about Gareth Hammond. He was dangerously attractive. He knew it, and she would be a fool not to admit it herself. The sensual molding of his mouth and the experienced appraisal in his eyes while they swept over her marked him as a man who knew and enjoyed women, in what he considered their *proper* place. She had seen that look in too many men's eyes before not to recognize it at once.

Her job marked her as an oddity in a heavily masculine world, and she was depressingly familiar with all the gambits designed to goad her into proving her femininity. Her strong sense of humor and her own confidence in her essential femininity had armored her against previous attempts at seduction, and she had found that the light touch was usually sufficient to turn away, harmlessly, the most persistent. Unfortunately, it didn't seem as though she would be able to use the light touch with Gareth Hammond. Whenever he came near her, she seemed to spit sparks like an arcing short, and the intensity of her reaction to him, negative though it was, surprised and disturbed her.

In spite of her comments to Tige on the unlikelihood of encountering Gareth in a social situation, it was just that which she feared. Her professionalism would be sufficient protection in any encounter with Mr. Hammond while she was working. Emotion was not intrusive while she was flying, and her mantle of cool detachment would effectively insulate her from the current of desire (?), attraction (?), or *whatever* it was that seemed to tingle over her skin whenever Gareth Hammond turned those green eyes on her. If she could confine her contact with him to the merely professional, she would be safe.

Safe! The word had no meaning around such a man. He was a predator, ready to gobble up unwary virgin tidbits with a snap of his flashing white teeth. She laughed at the image she had conjured up. She sat up abruptly. "Repeat after me three times, Morgain," she said aloud. "Who's afraid of the big bad wolf, the big bad wolf, the big bad wolf?" and in answer she chanted as she headed toward the back door, "Not I, not I, not I!"

CHAPTER II

When Tige came to collect her that evening she was nearly scintillating, full of vibrant energy and a zest for the coming encounter she somehow sensed in the offing. Her dress of turquoise cotton was peasant in derivation, baring her tanned shoulders and flaring out below the nipped-in waist to swirl in graceful folds below her trim ankles, alternately revealing and concealing the twisted natural leather of her sandals. Her eyes were a dark, glowing turquoise, glittering like jewels in her tanned face. Her honey-gold hair was piled atop her head, held in place by a silver and turquoise comb, and a turquoise pendant on a fine silver chain swung down to nestle just above the swell of her breasts, which rose from the embroidered neckline of the dress. The gold of her hair and skin and the faint coral of her lips were the only variations from the blazoned colors of turquoise and silver, and the total effect quite stunned Tige as he watched her glide toward him.

"Morgain, I'm speechless. Who needs wine tonight? I'm drunk on turquoise and silver."

"Ach, 'tis a silver tongue ye have, me lad, trying to turn a poor girl's head wi' your charming words." She dropped the accent and grinned up at him. "Let's go. I'm ready for one last fling before I start the grind again. Bring on the coach and horses; tomorrow I immerse myself in grease and gasoline instead of Chantilly."

Tige easily matched her mood, and the ride to the hotel was lighthearted, with all the enjoyment two healthy young people can generate when they are thoroughly at ease in each other's company. Morgain had dismissed all her forebodings and was determined to enjoy tonight and the companionship of the attractive man who was her escort. She was comfortable with Tige, and if there existed the possibility that he might truly fall in love with her, it had not happened yet, so she was free to indulge in the light flirtation they could both appreciate, knowing Tige would not read more into it than she meant. There would be no undignified grappling on the seat of the car when the time came for him to take her home. Tige was safe in the nicest sense of the word: not brotherly, but not loverlike either.

They walked arm in arm from the car park, and Tige gallantly opened the door for her, ushering her inside the hotel with a courtly, sweeping bow. She dropped him a mocking half curtsy and slid her arm through his again, laughing up at him as she did so.

She felt him stiffen slightly and half turned to follow the direction of his gaze, to encounter the steady, enigmatic sweep of two green eyes as they traveled with leisurely thoroughness up and down her body. A faint flush dyed her cheekbones, and her full lips tightened ever so slightly, but her eyes met the green ones steadily and coolly. With a serene inclination of her head she acknowledged the deep voice when it murmured, "Miss Kendrick, Tige," and her own "Mr. Hammond" was polite and neutral, not betraying the sudden heavy thud of the heartbeat she could feel shaking her rib cage.

With fatalistic calm Morgain waited for what was to come, surrendering to the sense of inevitability that had nagged her ever since John had let slip those key words, "He suggested you," in his office this morning. She had known then, as she knew now, that Gareth Hammond was on the hunt and she was the current quarry.

The look that passed between Tige and Morgain was almost telepathic in intensity, and Tige's reassuring grin so tickled her risibilities that her answering grin broke into a delighted gurgle of mirth. Gareth Hammond might discover that this road to seduction had more than a few bumps and detours along its course.

"I believe our table is waiting, Morgain. Gareth, good evening," Tige extricated them smoothly.

"Enjoy your dinner, Mr. Hammond. The food here is excellent" was Morgain's purring contribution.

As they swept into the dining room in the wake of the headwaiter, Tige bent his head toward Morgain and murmured, "Naughty, naughty. He's not one to take provocation lightly."

"Hmpf," was her unladylike sniff. "I don't imagine he's used to anything less than women falling for him like ninepins. Well, I never have been one for standing in line, and they do say that adversity is good for the soul. I don't plan to make myself answerable for Mr. Hammond's soul, but I'll be more than willing to supply the adversity."

She shook her head in dismay. "Tige, here we are again with Gareth Hammond as our sole topic of conversation. I won't have it. I do not wish to think or talk of that man. Exert your talents in social repartee and let us discuss something noncontroversial, religion or politics or something equally banal. Shall I regale you with more tales of the wicked life of an airline pilot? None firsthand experi-

41

ence, you understand, but guaranteed authentic nonetheless."

Morgain could feel the impact of Gareth Hammond's eyes between her shoulder blades throughout the excellent dinner. She had known when he entered the dining room, known without turning around. There was a cord of awareness stretched between them, and he had only to enter a room to tug all of her senses into cognizance of his presence. She wondered if she affected him the same way.

"The urge to rub the back of my neck is becoming almost irresistible, Tige." Her smile was rueful.

"I don't wonder" was his acknowledgment. "Shall we adjourn to the dance floor? I can rub your neck there and check to see if you have a hole bored in it at the same time."

Morgain gave a delighted giggle, and Tige beckoned for the waiter. He signed for the meal, assisted Morgain from her chair, and with a nod and a smile for the watching Gareth, they headed toward the room where the bar and the band were located.

"Now I know why some women have called him the panther," Tige grumbled. "He was looking at you like you were a tasty morsel staked out for his delectation. I've seen him escort a lot of women over the years I've known him, but I've never seen him look at another woman the way he looks at you."

"It's the added spice of the unattainable, Tige," Morgain assured him. "I'm nothing special, but he's the type to enjoy a challenge. If I had simpered at him and appeared to be bowled over by his charm, he'd have passed me by without a thought. Unfortunately, it's too late for such tactics to be effective and I'm not really the type for them anyway."

She shrugged a shapely shoulder. "If it weren't for John, I'd toss the whole thing up, but I can't let him down. Believe me, Tige, John is the only hold that Gareth Hammond has over me, and even that is not sufficient to get him anywhere when it comes to the bottom line. It may make things more protracted and uncomfortable, but three weeks isn't very long, and I think my powers of resistance are adequate for even the most determined assault over that length of time." She grinned reassuringly. "I'm a big girl now and nobody has been able to make me do something I didn't want to do for a long time."

They were dancing now, and she could see that Tige's face was serious and a little troubled.

"I've known Gareth ever since we were in college together. He graduated a year before I did, took over Hammond Enterprises from his father, and put it back on its feet. I came to work for him right after I graduated. I think I know him pretty well, and before this I would have sworn that he'd never use your friendship with John as a lever. He may be ruthless, but as long as I've known him I've never seen him anything but strictly fair and above-board. His women all knew the score and he's never gone after any other type. You know, we're building a lot of assumptions on not much data, but there's something between you . . . I could feel it from the first time I saw you together this afternoon."

He hesitated while he negotiated them around several wildly gyrating couples, and then continued, "Morgain, would it help if we pretended to be engaged or something?"

She was silent for a long minute, and then she shook her head. "Thanks for the offer, Tige, but when I do become engaged it will be for real. I can't use that sort of subter-

43

fuge, and on a more practical note, I don't think that Gareth would either believe, or pay attention to, any announcement of an engagement between us. We just don't give off that sort of spark when we're together"—Tige winced ostentatiously—"and he's entirely too perceptive not to sense it. I won't use you as a stalking horse and I won't give Mr. Hammond the satisfaction of using another man as a defense against him. All I ask is that you agree to testify as a character witness for me if I ever go on trial for murdering him."

He laughed and hugged her close. "That's my girl. I'll put my money on you every time, Morgain my dear." A slow grin curved his mouth. "You know, I have a feeling that if you decide you want him, I think you could be the one to drop the noose around Gareth's neck."

"Well, I don't want him," she responded tartly. "I just want to get through these next three weeks. Gareth is not my beau ideal, nor is he likely to be. . . ." She reached up to rub the back of her neck and then stiffened when she realized what she was doing.

Tige laughed and nodded. "Yep, he just came in and he's heading this way. I think he plans to join us at the table. Are you sure you don't want to become engaged to me?" he teased her gently.

She shot him a look that could have shriveled him in his tracks and then laughed in her turn. "It would serve you right if I did. You're a good friend, Tige, too good to wish me on you as a wife or even a fiancée."

His face shadowed momentarily, and he said softly, "There was a time . . . ," and then he continued more briskly, "but I have a well developed sense of self-preservation and I know better than to place myself squarely

44

between an irresistible force and the old immovable object."

"Which is which?" she questioned him with a twinkle in her eyes.

"You're each a bit of both, and I shall remove myself to the sidelines to watch the coming conflict from safety," he said firmly. "Let me know if we still have a dinner date tomorrow night after the end of the first skirmish."

He deftly steered her back toward their table, where Gareth had pulled up a chair and now lounged at his ease. As they approached he rose with fluid grace and held Morgain's chair ready for her. She thanked him for the courtesy with a brief and formal smile and settled herself placidly at the table. A waiter approached, and the order for drinks was given. Gareth raised an eyebrow at Morgain's request for ginger ale.

"I'm a working girl tomorrow, Mr. Hammond," she answered the look with composure. "I follow the rule of 'No smoking within twelve hours of a flight and no alcohol within fifty feet of an aircraft,' except that I don't smoke at all."

Tige chuckled, and Gareth's white smile flashed in the dimness. "I'm glad to see that you're sedulous in the performance of your job, Morgain," Gareth approved mockingly.

Her eyes flashed but her voice was even and cool as she replied. "I am *very* serious about my job, Mr. Hammond. My employers expect professionalism and I make sure they get it."

His eyes narrowed, and the line of his jaw was suddenly taut. Morgain felt her throat go dry. She was relieved when the waiter appeared from the dimness and placed a frosty glass before her. She picked up the glass and al-

45

lowed the astringent coolness to trickle slowly down her throat, to ease the sudden sense of constriction. When she was sure she could trust her voice, she turned to Gareth and said,

"Getting the Buckeye contract from the government was quite an achievement. I understand that it will be a very sizable complex by the time it's completed. Your company will coordinate not only the actual construction of the physical plant but also the installation of the electronic equipment, isn't that correct?"

"Yes, it is, Morgain," he followed her lead smoothly. "In fact, the physical plant is about three quarters completed by now, which is why we signed the contract with John to begin ferrying in the electronic equipment, as well as the technicians who will see to its installation and, later, the scientists who will calibrate and eventually use it. You'll be carrying some highly expensive cargo when the flights begin."

His smile was wolfish, and she didn't miss the faint emphasis on the "you'll" or the waiting stillness while he gave her time to protest once again that John and Ken would be responsible for Buckeye.

Her gaze was limpid and guileless. She ignored the opening. "I haven't really paid too much attention to the project, so I'm rather vague on the details. Why fly so much in? There is a road that leads there, isn't there? I know it's totally isolated, but can't most of the equipment go in by road? From what John said, we'll be flying in daily consignments at least. That's a lot of equipment and a pretty expensive way to transport it."

Tige laughed. "There's a road all right, but it's a road in name only. We did transport the construction equipment that way, but if the electronic gear went by that

46

route, I don't think it would be of much use when it finally arrived. Even padded and cushioned it wouldn't survive the rigors of that road."

"Neither would the techs and scientists," Gareth put in with a chuckle. "Those that I've met so far are anything but the outdoor type, and two hundred miles of heat, dust, and washboard road would jostle them into catatonia. Nope, Buckeye requires air service daily, right now, and even when it's a going concern, John will find Buckeye a most profitable source of business."

"John will earn every penny of it, believe me. Those mountains aren't any picnic to fly in, and the downdrafts in the canyon approach to Buckeye are the trickiest I've ever encountered," Morgain averred with some heat.

Gareth eyed her with some surprise, and a small frown furrowed his forehead. "I hadn't realized. Just how dangerous is it?"

"It isn't . . . *if* you know what you're doing. It's no place for an amateur, or someone with just a hundred hours of flight time"—she gave him a sweetly malicious smile—"but an experienced, competent pilot won't have any real problem."

She was surprised to discern a faint flush on Gareth's face, and Tige took a sudden large sip of his drink, which seemed to go down the wrong way. Gareth gave them both an ominous look that Tige missed, as he was still in a paroxysm of coughing, and Morgain ignored, feeling that the honors belonged to her, for this round at least.

Tige, convinced that a diversion was essential at this point, stifled his cough and asked Morgain to dance. She accepted without unseemly alacrity, but the look she tossed him was grateful. When he whirled her onto the dance floor she caught a glimpse of Gareth watching them as he lifted his drink to his lips. His expression was imperturbable, but the eyes that watched her over the rim of his glass glowed with a deep inner fire. She shivered.

"Deliberately baiting the animals can be dangerous." Tige murmured in her ear.

She was apologetic. "I didn't start out to do it. Believe me, it was the furthest thing from my mind." She wrinkled her nose penitently at him. "The devil made me do it!"

"And the devil is liable to make you pay for it," was his quelling retort.

The music ended much too soon to suit Morgain, but she was no coward. She didn't suggest that they spend the rest of the evening on the dance floor. Gareth rose as they approached the table, and the gleam in his eye warned her that his time had come. Before she had a chance to sit, his hand slid beneath her elbow and he drew her to his side.

"May I have the pleasure of this next dance, Morgain?"

"Of course, Mr. Hammond," she purred sweetly.

His fingers clamped firmly on her elbow, and she knew that a fraction more pressure would be bruising. Tige shot her a monitory look, but there was a rebellious glitter in her eyes when Gareth led her out into the swirling throng. He pulled her firmly into his embrace, and she found herself automatically responding to his expert lead.

"I think it's about time you called me Gareth."

It was a command, not a request, and Morgain's immediate impulse was to answer, "Yes, Mr. Hammond," but the memory of those steel-strong fingers holding her elbow deterred her. Morgain might justly be called stubborn, but she was not foolhardy.

"All right, Gareth. You may call me Morgain."

His chuckle was rich and prolonged. "You little hellcat. You'll be the devil to tame."

Morgain seethed. Judging her time with cool precision, she chose a moment when the momentum of the dance gave her a weight and balance advantage. She tromped hard on Gareth's right foot. The breath hissed sharply through his lips, and she raised innocent blue eyes to his furious green ones.

"Oh, I'm *so* sorry. Did I step on your foot? I'm a little out of practice. I'll try to do better next time," she promised sweetly.

The music ended as she finished speaking, but they both knew that it wasn't the next dance she referred to. She led the way from the floor, heading toward the table, but just before they reached it, Gareth slowed the pace and murmured in her ear, "I suppose I should be thankful that you're not addicted to spike heels."

Morgain smiled seductively up at him. "I've always thought that they were very flattering to a woman's legs. Perhaps I'll invest in a pair."

Tige caught the tail end of the conversation and asked Morgain curiously, "Invest in a pair of what?"

"Spike heels. Gareth and I were discussing women's shoe styles," Morgain purred, and bared her teeth in a smile. "Gareth doesn't favor that type of shoe. I think he feels that they're too hard on the feet."

Gareth tipped a mocking salute, and Tige led her back onto the dance floor, his face a study in bewilderment.

"What in the world is going on? How ever did you and Gareth begin a discussion of women's shoe styles?"

"It was merely an association of ideas," she explained airily. "He called me a hellcat and I accidentally stepped on his foot while we were dancing."

"I don't want to hear any more," Tige groaned. "What

49

time is it? Is it late enough so that I can gracefully take you home, before you and Gareth come to blows?"

"I'm sure it wouldn't come to that," she soothed him. "I'm positive Gareth would never hit a lady."

"How's that supposed to help you?" he retorted dryly.

"Ouch. Well, I suppose I deserved that one." She ostentatiously smothered a yawn. "My, my. It certainly has been a *long* day and I'm sooo tired. I hate to break up the evening, Tige, dear, but could you take me home?"

"At last, vestiges of common sense. Come on, pet. Let's make our adieux and retire from the field, bloody but unbowed. I'll take you home. Then I'm going to soothe my shattered nerves with a good stiff Scotch!"

As they rode home in the car Tige questioned her. "May I safely assume that we have a dinner date tomorrow night?"

"Are you sure you still want to take me out?" Morgain retorted with asperity. "I was beginning to feel that you considered my vicinity had all the charm of the fallout zone around a hydrogen bomb blast."

"Tut, tut, my child," Tige admonished her, "Reserve your fire. I'm a noncombatant, remember? I'll pick you up at six again, unless you call me and tell me otherwise after you talk to John tomorrow. I'll find some dark, secluded spot where *no one* would think to look for us."

She smiled at him in apology. "I'm sorry, Tige. I didn't mean to snap at you. A dinner *à deux* will be just the thing, even if it's at the local hamburger heaven, as long as it is *à deux*."

"Hmmm, I hadn't thought of Hippo's," he commented, "but now that you mention it, I'm sure no one would look for us there. Do you prefer cheese on your burgers, and what flavor of shake strikes your fancy?"

"Idiot." They walked to the front door, hand in hand, and she said, seriously, as she prepared to open the door, "Thank you for the dinner, Tige. I did truly enjoy it, and even the dancing afterward had its moments." A gurgle of mirth leaked out. "It did indeed have its moments!"

He kissed her on the forehead and shook his head. "I can almost find it within myself to feel sorry for Gareth."

The next afternoon Morgain stopped in John's office after completing her flights for the day. She was tired, sweaty, and stiff. Small light aircraft do not enjoy the amenities of air conditioning or deluxe padded pilot's seats, and cleaning up after an airsick passenger is liable to fray the most equable temper. Morgain did not claim to have an equable temper.

She glared at John while he dictated into a handheld Dictaphone. When he had concluded and switched it off, she fixed him with a level stare and in dulcet tones inquired as to the location of his suggestion box. He eyed her with some trepidation and wanted to know why she asked.

"Because I have a suggestion for you, John, dear," she cooed.

"Welll," he drawled, "actually I sent it out to be painted yesterday. Can I treat you to a cold soft drink? Dare I ask how your first day back among the peons was?" John grinned at her and led her to the soft-drink machine. He dropped money in the slot and gestured widely. "Choose your poison."

Morgain chuckled. "You know what I miss most, John? The flight attendants. It's beneath my dignity to clean up after a passenger who missed the barf bag." She tilted her head back and let half the contents of the bottle flow down her throat. "Ahh, I may live after all. Well, John, what

51

cow pasture are you sending me to tomorrow?" She took another deep swallow.

John shifted his feet and cleared his throat. Morgain removed the bottle from her lips and regarded him thoughtfully. "Well, John?" she repeated even more softly.

"Ahem." John developed an all-consuming interest in the nonexistent shine of his battered boots. He glanced up at her and dropped his gaze again. "Morgain . . ." he began, and seemed to run out of words.

She sighed. "Never mind, John. Let me tell you. Due to circumstances beyond your control I'll be going into Buckeye tomorrow. *¿No es verdad?*" She drained the rest of the bottle and hefted it speculatively, but he could tell her mind was far away. She looked at the bottle and then gently replaced it in the rack beside the other empties. Her eyes focused on him once again, and she smiled. "It's okay, I expected it." She became briskly practical. "When is the show time and what are we hauling?" They became engrossed in technicalities, and he let out a soundless breath of relief.

Morgain soaked and soaped long and lovingly in her hot tub, frothing with bubble bath oil. Her hair was restored to its gleaming luster by shampoo, and after it was blown dry, she piled it softly atop her head in its customary style to leave her neck cool and bare for the evening. As she left the bathroom, wrapped in a voluminous towel, she met her mother in the hall.

"Hi, Mom. How are Jenny and Jeremy? I told Ken that Tige and I would stop by for a moment this evening before dinner to show off my new and only nephew. Does Jenny really feel up to visitors, even quick ones? It's her first full

52

day home from the hospital, after all. Ken claims she's bouncing with rude health and says he's going to send her back out in the rice fields right away, but what do men know?"

"Though I wouldn't recommend the rice fields, she's more than able to take you and Tige in stride," her mother assured her. "Drop by, by all means; Jeremy is just beautiful. . . . I'm sure he smiled at me today when I changed his diaper."

"How marvelous; when I saw him yesterday, before they left the hospital, he wouldn't even open his eyes. Is he walking yet? Children do grow up so fast." Morgain's tones were dry, but her eyes sparkled and her grin was infectious.

"All grandmothers are allowed to dote and gloat," her mother responded with spurious dignity and an equally wide grin. "How did your day go, Morgain, dear?"

"Hot, sweaty, and stinky!" her daughter rejoined succinctly. "One of the passengers got airsick—"

"Oh, dear." There was a pause. "Where are you and Tige going for dinner?"

"Hippo's." Morgain chortled at the expression on her mother's face. "But Mom, it used to be one of my favorite places. Perhaps I'm trying to regain my lost youth."

"Poor old lady you. Hippo's. Really?"

"No, not really. At least I don't think so. Tige just suggested I name some places where we would be unlikely to run into Gareth, and Hippo's came naturally to mind. It'll be another early night, anyway. Tomorrow we start the Buckeye flights and I have to supervise all the stowing of the first load of equipment. Heaven help us if the stuff starts to shift in flight. At least electronic equipment

53

doesn't get airsick, though I have a load of techs scheduled for the second flight."

"You're starting to shiver. Go get into some clothes," her mother ordered her absently. She followed her daughter into the bedroom and perched on the bed as Morgain began to pull on her underclothes. "Are you going to be taking the Buckeye flights, dear? I thought John and Ken were going to take them."

Morgain laughed shortly. " 'The best laid schemes o' mice and men/gang aft a-gley.' I have, by special request, been designated to handle them."

She began to dress swiftly in a soft green knitted top, trimmed in white at neck and sleeves and embroidered with white daisy motifs in a random spray. She slid into a silky white half-slip and covered it with a swinging, pleated, short white skirt. Tiny enameled ear studs in the shape of a daisy, and a matching ring, were her only jewelry, and comfortable white thong-strapped sandals finished her preparations. She thrust lipstick, wallet, and comb into a small white straw bag and met her mother's eyes.

"It's all right. I didn't blow up all over John. To tell you the truth, I was expecting it, especially after last night. I didn't get a chance to tell you, but I had another run-in with Gareth." Her lips curved in a reminiscent smile. "I wonder how his foot was this morning?" In explanation she continued, "He said something that . . . ah . . . irritated me, and I accidentally happened to step on his foot while we were dancing." Her eyes flared green. "Tame me, would he," she muttered.

Just then the doorbell pealed, and Morgain glanced at the clock. "Whoops, I didn't realize it was so late. That'll be Tige." She dropped a fond kiss on her mother's cheek and left with a swirl of skirt to let Tige in. She pulled the door open as the bell pealed again and remonstrated, "You must be starving, Ti . . ." Her voice trailed away on an indrawn breath as she looked up into amused green eyes.

"You're not Tige," she said idiotically. Recovering slightly, she hastened on, "I mean, where's Tige?" and a shade less graciously, "I mean, what are *you* doing here?"

"You dither charmingly, Morgain. May I come in?"

She stiffened and clutched the half-opened door more firmly, as if to be sure he wouldn't thrust it open and enter in spite of her. She surveyed him from head to foot, from shining black hair, down wide shoulders covered by a light blue knitted shirt, past long legs covered by close-fitting dark blue slacks, to end with polished black half-boots. While she made her survey he hooked his thumbs in the belt loops of his slacks and waited for her to meet his eyes again.

"Why?" she questioned with bald candor. "I have a date," she continued.

"I know," he agreed smoothly, "but is this"—he gestured at the porch—"really the place to discuss it?"

Conceding the point, she opened the door fully and preceded him into the hall. "Do come in, Gareth," she drawled provocatively as she led the way into the living room. She stopped in the middle of the room and turned to face him, only to discover that he had followed her so closely that she was confronting his broad chest at a distance of less than a foot. She stepped back rapidly, and his hands shot out to grasp her shoulders to save her, perhaps, from overbalancing. His hands were hard and warm, and the thumbs lay along the line of her collarbones on the soft skin left bare by the scoop neck of her knitted top. For a protracted moment those strong hands held her, and as they withdrew the thumbs dragged caressingly across the skin until his hands fell away to his sides.

Her head came up like a startled deer, and she lifted turquoise eyes to clash with his green ones head on. She took another, more balanced, step backward and indicated a nearby armchair, inviting him to sit down. He waited until she had seated herself and then accepted the proffered chair.

Morgain could still feel the warm drag of his thumbs across her skin and resisted the temptation to look down to see if there were visible signs of his touch in addition to the residual tingle he had left behind. She knew her cheeks still bore a faint wild flush . . . she could feel their heat . . . and to mask her reaction she spoke with as much chill composure as she could muster.

"What have we to discuss, Gareth?"

"I am, alas, the bearer of sad tidings," he said with no evidence of sorrow. "Unfortunately, Tige will be unable to keep his dinner date with you. There was a sudden crisis in the San Francisco office, and knowing his recent penchant for trips to San Francisco, I felt sure that he was the perfect man to deal with it." He regarded her blandly.

Morgain drew in a deep breath, torn between fury and unwilling amusement. Her teeth clenched over the impulsive sarcastic retort that sprang to mind, and she smiled with sweetness, glancing thoughtfully at the right foot that he had propped casually over his left knee when he leaned back in comfort in the chair.

"What a shame, but I do understand Tige's devotion to duty. It must be very reassuring to have such competent and dedicated people to depend on." She rose gracefully from her chair, bringing him to his feet in response. "It was thoughtful of you to come by to let me know. I'm sure few employers would be so considerate of their employees' interests. Did you say how long you thought Tige might be away?"

She began moving toward the door but was forestalled when her mother and father entered suddenly, her father having just gotten home from work.

"Morgain," said her mother in surprise, "I thought you and Tige had left. Oh!" She suddenly realized that it was not Tige who had moved to stand beside her daughter. She looked at Morgain in inquiry.

Morgain smiled tightly. "There was a slight problem. Tige had to go to San Francisco suddenly. Mom and Dad, this is Gareth Hammond. Gareth, my parents, Mr. and Mrs. Kendrick." Hands were shaken and greetings murmured. Morgain continued, "Mr. Hammond was kind enough to come by to tell me personally of Tige's sudden change in plans."

Gareth had resumed his place by Morgain, and now he smiled down at her. "It was the least I could do. I feel somewhat responsible because Tige was sent to San Francisco on my business." Morgain nearly choked over this shameless effrontery, and she almost missed Gareth's next words. "Since Morgain's invitation to dinner was disrupted because of me, I felt it was only fair that I take Tige's place."

Had Morgain been able to force a sound through her throat, she would have laughed hysterically. Through a swirling red fog she heard Gareth reiterate how much he had enjoyed meeting her parents as he grasped her hand firmly in his.

"We'd better leave now, Morgain. I know you have an

57

early start tomorrow, and I don't want to keep you out too late tonight."

She was swept out the door and inserted in Gareth's car, and he was reversing down the drive before the stupor left her. She whirled in the seat to face him.

In furious accents she hissed at him, "Take me back to the house this minute, Gareth."

"I thought for a moment you were going to call me Mr. Hammond again. How wise of you not to, Morgain, my love," his deep voice mocked.

"I'll call you anything I please, Gareth Hammond, and don't you call me 'my love.' I'm not your love. I'm not your anything. Take me back home!" she spat.

"But I'd like you to be." His voice was alight with humor and smooth with assurance. "You will be, you know."

She fell back against the seat in shock. The absurdity of the situation overwhelmed her and she began to laugh. "You are too preposterous to be true," she gasped out.

"*L'audace. L'audace. Toujours l'audace,*" he quoted. "I want you, Morgain. I see no reason not to say it."

"Wanting is not having," she snapped, and then blushed fiery red when he laughed.

"Well said." He grinned at her, his eyes sweeping over her flushed countenance.

Trying another tack, Morgain gritted at him, "Well, I don't want you."

"I will make you want me, Morgain," his assurance was calmly spoken.

"Take me back this instant. I will not have dinner with you, and John or no John, I will not fly one piece of equipment or one person into Buckeye for you. You can carry them piggyback to Buckeye before I will lift a finger

58

for you." Morgain's breath came unevenly, and her eyes were narrowed with fury.

"Have you no faith in your powers of resistance?" he taunted her. "Are you afraid that you will indeed come to want me and so you've decided to run away?"

Morgain had thought she had already reached the pinnacle of fury, but these latest words so enraged her that she went icy cold. Her brain, under the stimulus of his provocation, conceived a plan, stunning in its simplicity and diabolical cunning. He wanted her, did he? Well, she would drive him mad with wanting. She would lead him on, subtly promising, seeming to be attracted to him against her will, nearly surrendering to his overwhelming attraction, and then . . . denouement. The final curtain would come down with her speech telling him what she really thought of him.

She turned her head to look at him with steady eyes. "I'm not afraid of any man, Gareth, and I'm perfectly safe with you. You're not the type to take a woman by force. Your ego demands a willing surrender, and that makes me safe. You may make me furious, but I'll never fear you. I'll fly your Buckeye runs and I'll even go out to dinner with you tonight." Now it was her turn to smile with assurance. "Where are we going to eat? Suddenly I've developed a tremendous appetite. I only had half a sandwich and a carton of milk for lunch."

"I thought we'd go to the Rib Barn. Barbecue is very filling, and you don't look like a girl who objects to eating with her fingers. You're a very adaptable person, I think."

"Thank you, I think. The Rib Barn is fine. I try to eat there at least once every time I come home to visit. Their spareribs are delicious, and I've never found any as good anywhere else. By the way, can we make a small detour before we eat? I promised Jenny, my sister-in-law, that Tige and I would drop by for a minute before dinner. I wanted to show off my new nephew. Since you're taking Tige's place, perhaps you'll deputize for him there, too?"

She gave him directions for reaching Ken and Jenny's after his nod of acquiescence, and continued, "Jeremy, my nephew, was the unwitting cause of our first meeting, as I'm sure you remember."

His lips twitched, and he said, "Yes. I was rude and you were insolent. A fair exchange all around. I might have turned you over my knee if I hadn't been already over an hour late for an important meeting."

"You might have tried," she agreed sweetly.

An hour later they sat ensconced at a table laid with a red and white checkered cloth and burdened by plates of succulent ribs. There were side dishes of crisp fried onion rings and tangy baked ranch-style beans, a covered basket of hot French bread, and frost-beaded mugs of golden pale beer. Morgain surveyed the feast happily and picked up the first juicy rib.

As she bit into it with a sigh of pure pleasure, Gareth observed, "Your bib is slipping." He deftly adjusted it, managing to caress the side of her neck in the process. She rapped his knuckles smartly with the rib bone as his hand withdrew, and he sucked the sauce off his knuckles and eyed her warily. She finished stripping the meat off the bone and used her napkin delicately to remove the sauce from the corners of her mouth.

"The ribs are delicious. Don't you think so, Gareth?" she drawled with gentle malice.

"The sauce certainly is, my love." He picked up a rib of his own and bit into it. Morgain was a quick learner. She didn't comment on his endearment, except to vow to

60

herself that someday he'd use them in earnest. The pile of discarded bones and used moist towelettes grew, and the conversation was sporadic for quite a while afterward. Finally Gareth and Morgain wiped the sauce from their fingers for the last time and gave mutual sighs of repletion.

"Marvelous! Whenever I come here I always wonder if we'll ever get through all those ribs, but somehow we always manage. I'll admit, though, that this time it was a near thing on my part." She grinned at him in happy camaraderie.

"I don't know where you put it all, but you're quite a trencherman for such a little slip of a thing. You must have cost your parents a pretty penny in grocery bills when you still lived at home. No wonder they were so happy to see someone take you out to dinner," Gareth teased.

"Were they happy? You hustled me out so quickly that I didn't notice. As to being a little slip of a thing, I'm five feet seven in my bare feet, but I'll be happy to allow you poetic license."

He seized the opening at once. "What else will you allow me, Morgain, darling?"

Her seductive smile stopped the breath in his throat and she purred softly, "Not a damn thing, Gareth, darling."

"That smile is a potent weapon, my love. Be careful how and where you use it. It could backfire on you and accomplish something you hadn't planned for." His look was explicit. "By the way, I'll be flying with you to Buckeye tomorrow morning. I'll ride out when you ferry the equipment and come back with you after you've brought in the technicians on the second load. I want to check out the unloading procedures, and some problems have cropped up that I have to handle personally, but I should be through by the time you're ready to start back."

"All right, Gareth. We start loading at 0730 sharp. That means I have an 0630 show time," she added with unsubtle intent.

"How tactfully put." He reached for her hand and captured her wrist, holding it in a gentle but unbreakable grip. "Before we go, I want you to promise me you'll have dinner with me tomorrow night."

She knew he could feel the sudden accelerated throb of her pulse as his forefinger stroked the soft inner skin of her wrist. He held her eyes with his, and the message in them was serious and not a little questioning, as though he was suddenly puzzled by an unfamiliar sensation. When she failed to answer, he gently loosened his grasp on her wrist and trailed a caress across her lax palm as he released her from all physical contact.

He spread his empty palms face up, and his smile was wry. "No pressure, no coercion. I would very much enjoy the pleasure of your company for dinner tomorrow night. Will you come?"

"Yes, I will."

He smiled. "Led but not driven, eh?"

"And sometimes not even led," she warned him.

"I have the message," he assured her. "I'll just have to be very careful that you don't realize I'm trying to lead you where I want you to go."

Her husky gurgle of laughter wrapped around him as he stood behind her, ready to assist her from her chair. His fingers flexed, and the flare of desire in his eyes as he looked down at the top of her bright head would have sent hot color to her cheeks had she chanced to intercept that glance. He was finding it increasingly difficult to subdue the impulse to stroke that silken skin, and the imagined taste of those laughing lips had formed the subject of several dreams of the type he had thought behind him, along with his adolescence.

He enjoyed the company of women, but found that familiarity bred, if not contempt, at least boredom. Women came easily to him, drawn by physical desire and the aura of power that was an integral part of his personality, but though he knew many beautiful and intelligent women, he had found none who could exert more than a momentary pull on his senses. He considered the possibility that Morgain's inaccessibility was a great part of the allure she had, but easily rejected this theory after a moment's reflection. There had been other women whose pursuit, for one reason or another, would have required considerable effort, and he had turned away from them without a moment's hesitation.

Morgain was . . . Morgain . . . like no other woman he had ever met, and he was being forced into the unpalatable realization that she was rapidly becoming an obsession with him. Well, he could cure himself. Once he had possessed her, he would be free again, unhaunted by the sound of her voice as it laughed or argued with him. He would satiate himself with the taste and feel the scent of her and therein would lie his release.

Morgain walked beside Gareth to the car and wondered what had placed that grim and somber shade across his face. A muscle ticked in his jaw, and his eyes were shuttered in a hooded, brooding introspection. He assisted her into the car with impersonal courtesy and began the drive home in silence.

The silence lasted all the way to the driveway of her parents' home. By now Morgain was thoroughly puzzled and not a little wary. Gareth shut off the car's engine with a snap of his wrist that threatened to break the key in the lock. The face he turned toward her bore the expression of a man driven near the limits of his endurance. She began to fumble desperately with the clasp of her seat belt.

"Th . . . thank you for the dinner, Gareth. I'll see you tomorrow morning at the field—"

Her words were cut off in a gasp as he pulled her into his arms and swooped down on her mouth. From the speed of his descent she was expecting a brutal, ravaging kiss, but his lips when they covered hers were tender and warmly wooing. They sipped and tantalized, leading her to respond in spite of herself. For several heady moments they were lost in sweet mutual exploration, and when Gareth's lips left hers to travel over her cheeks and eyelids, her mouth instinctively and blindly sought his for a renewal of that exquisite delight. She had kissed and been kissed before, but never had she experienced such a compelling escalation of desire. As his lips began to travel down the arch of her throat and his hands sought familiarity with the curves of her body, sanity surfaced for a brief moment and she jerked herself out of his arms and over to her side of the car.

"Stop it, Gareth," she panted. Her hand raised slowly to fend him off, but he didn't move toward her, merely lifted his arms to invite her back into his compelling embrace.

"Come here, Morgain, my little golden witch." His voice was low and beguiling. The temptation to give in to the promise offered by those enfolding arms was almost overwhelming. In them she would find heaven and desire's fulfillment. "Come back to me, Morgain. Let me love you. My arms are empty without you in them. Come here, my love." The last words were a mere whisper, but they were as effective as a shout. Passion was doused like a match dropped into water, and her brain regained its overriding detachment.

"Oh, no, Gareth." She forced amusement into her voice, firmly ignoring its tendency to quaver. "I'm not your love. You have no love to offer me. You offer me passion and desire, but they are not love, only its counterfeit. What you offer me tarnishes and dies, leaving a sour taste in the mouth. Real love, the only kind I'll ever settle for, doesn't die, and the taste is full and sweet, with no bitter aftermath. The more you have of it, the more you want. It satisfies but doesn't satiate."

With a dexterous twist of her body she opened her door and slid lithely out in one flowing motion. She bent slightly, and her words came quietly to him—"Good night, Gareth. I'll see you tomorrow morning"—and she was gone, a sable shadow in the night. He saw only a faint, momentary lightening of the darkness when she opened the front door and slipped inside.

CHAPTER III

Morgain stood quietly for a moment in the dimness of the hall, thankful that her mother had stopped leaving the porch and hall lights on for her once she had turned nineteen. She went into the small powder room off the hall and flicked on the light. In the mirror she saw a heavy-eyed face whose lips bore the unmistakable stamp of passion on their pouting fullness. Her hair was tumbled around her shoulders, and with a wry grin she hoped Gareth had fun gathering up the hairpins that would be scattered over the front seat of his car. With luck he might even manage to sit on one or two.

She began a swift repair of her appearance, starting with a splash of cold water to drive away the sensuous drowsiness engendered by his lovemaking. She reapplied lip gloss and used some hairpins she found in the medicine cabinet to effect a renewal of the hairstyle she had started the evening with. The overall effect was pretty good, she told herself, and if she could not meet the eyes of the girl in the mirror with candor, for fear of what she would see revealed in the dark turquoise depths, that was a problem she'd come to grips with later.

With convincing casualness she sauntered out into the family room, where her mother sat crocheting and her father was engrossed in a crossword puzzle as the stereo released the liquid strains of Mancini. They both looked up and smiled, and her mother patted the couch in invitation.

"Okay, Mom, but just for a minute. I have a 0630 show time tomorrow and it's already been a long day. Well, now that you've seen him in the flesh, what do you think of Gareth Hammond?"

He's certainly an attractive man," replied her mother cautiously. "Rather forceful, though. Did he actually ask you to go out to dinner with him? Somehow I got the impression that you were somewhat bemused when he . . . er . . . escorted you out the door."

Mother and daughter shared a glance of feminine understanding.

"Shall we say that the invitation was an informal one?" was Morgain's dry rejoinder. "You understand, of course, that he sent Tige away deliberately. Gareth Hammond is rude, arrogant, and entirely too sure of himself, and if I had a lick of sense, I'd avoid him like the Black Death."

"Do you think he'd let you?" her father contributed with sudden insight. Mother and daughter turned to regard him with surprise, as though an oracle had suddenly spoken. "Chick, he's a very determined man and used to accomplishing what he sets his mind on. I'll now give you a piece of masculine, fatherly advice that you are at liberty to accept or reject. If you truly want nothing to do with the man, forget about helping John and run like the devil was chasing you." He then returned to contemplation of his crossword with perfect equanimity.

Morgain's mother sighed and remarked to her daughter, "Even after thirty years of marriage to your father, there are times when I long to throw something at him, especially when he has such an irritating way of being right. My dear, your father and I have great faith in your judgment, but I don't imagine that men like Gareth come along very often. You'll go your own way in the end, and that's as it should be, but remember that there's no shame in cutting your losses and retiring from the field. And above all, don't let Grandfather Ryan's temper goad you into doing something you might regret in calmer moments." She leaned forward to pat her daughter's unconsciously clenched hand. "End of motherly advice, and now, off to bed with you. A sleepy pilot is a poor pilot," she announced with a twinkle in her eye and the air of one announcing a newly discovered pearl of wisdom.

"Yes, Mother, dear," responded her daughter with suspect meekness and docility. She dropped a fond kiss on her father's cheek and hugged her mother briefly. As she started out the door, her mother stopped her with a question.

"Will you be in for dinner tomorrow evening, dear?"

Morgain's eyes glinted as a slow smile curved her mouth. "It all depends, but I rather suspect not. No, I think not. Good night, all."

Morgain went into the bedroom where she had passed her girlhood and surveyed the room with unseeing eyes. She undressed mechanically, pulled on her nightgown, and went into the bathroom to remove her makeup and brush her hair and teeth. She completed the nightly ritual automatically and returned to her room. She climbed into the bed where she had dreamed so many girlish dreams and wept the easy, sometimes bitter, tears of adolescence. The sun-dried scent of the clean sheets was familiar, as was the pattern of shadow and light cast by the honeysuckle vine that draped softly around her window.

She stretched with a long, muscle-arching pull and clasped her hands behind her head. She was used to assessing problems dispassionately and methodically; her profession demanded it, and when unclouded by temper, her brain was incisive and analytical. She wasn't at all sure, however, that she was going to be able to consider Gareth dispassionately, no matter how hard she tried. Whenever she thought of him and the kisses they had shared—for she was honest enough to admit that she was a more than willing participant—a melting fire ran through her veins to tingle all the way to the ends of her fingers and toes.

The first fact she had to face was that her plan to lead Gareth on was going to have to be scrapped immediately! That sort of thing only worked when one could retain control of one's emotions, and Gareth had conclusively demonstrated tonight that he could pull a response from her, be she willing or not.

She sighed. It had been a lovely, lovely plan, and she regretted having to give it up. It would have been *most* satisfying to give him a big fat jolt in the ego. Well, there was no help for it . . . she'd be the one to receive the jolt if she were foolish enough to tangle with Gareth on that basis, and her mother hadn't raised a foolish daughter.

As far as she could see, that left her with two alternatives: flight or fight. If she cut her vacation short, she would leave John in the lurch and it would be an admission to Gareth that she feared his influence over her so much that her only defense was to cravenly run away.

No! She shot up in bed, her fists clenched. The thought of his mocking green eyes and knowing smile, should she choose that course, were enough to dispose of that alternative without further consideration. She had told him tonight that she feared no man, and it was still true. She was not afraid of *him,* she was afraid of herself. That realization calmed her and showed her the course of action she must follow. She could see Gareth, even go out with him, as long as she could avoid situations where he could use his potent physical magnetism to overwhelm her defenses.

She would armor herself with the knowledge that while Gareth did in fact desire her, she was not the first nor would she be the last woman he pursued. He could give her heaven for a time, but inevitably the time would come when he would move on to the next conquest and she would be left with hell.

"I'll be the one who got away, Gareth," she vowed softly in the darkness of her room, and turned over to fall into dreamless sleep.

The next morning Morgain rose in the dark and crept softly into the bathroom, careful not to disturb her parents. She showered quickly and applied her makeup with a light and expert hand. Her golden, tanned skin needed no blusher, and her eyes glowed with a luster and militant sparkle that needed no cosmetic aid. She'd not only be the one who got away, she'd do it with verve and style.

She considered her hair for a long moment and then pulled it it softly back from her face, allowing it to tumble in a silken cascade down the back of her neck and shoulders. She slipped into pale blue, crisp cotton duck slacks that flared slightly at the ankle, and topped them with a softly patterned shirt in shades of blues and cream that she knew from experience would look cool and unwilted, no matter what the temperature. She then tucked a scent-soaked cotton ball into her bra, between her breasts. The heat of her body would release the light floral fragrance

71

continuously throughout the day without further application of scent.

Back in her room again, she slipped into white terry tennis socks and laced up a pair of low-cut pale blue canvas tennis shoes. They were practical for this type of flying, even though they lacked the coolness of sandals. After checking to be sure that she had everything she needed safely stowed in her small canvas shoulder bag, she made a quick foray to the kitchen to annex a banana and an orange. Then she slipped silently out of the front door to the car she used when she was at home. If her mother needed it during the day, her father could take her by the airfield to collect it, and Ken would drop her off on his way home.

Morgain neatly disposed of the banana as she drove through the quiet, deserted streets, but saved the orange until she reached the airfield. Dawn had paled the sky by the time she parked and locked the car. She waved at the two men who were trundling a loaded trolly toward the waiting plane. They would not start stowing the cargo until she was there to supervise, so she quickened her step and entered the building housing John's offices.

The waiting room was deserted, but the coffeepot was full, so she poured herself a steaming cup of black mud, added sugar and milk, and entered the inner office with no more than a perfunctory knock. John and Gareth were deep in consultation, so she walked over to John's cluttered desk and extracted the latest weather reports, waved her coffee cup in silent greeting, and returned to the outer office. There she pulled one of the folding chairs next to the table at comfortable angle. She sat, placed her cup beside her, and with the weather reports spread on her lap, leaned back in the chair and propped her feet on the table, ankles casually crossed. She sipped and read for several minutes until she felt the familiar sensation on the back of her neck that told her Gareth was watching, whereupon she looked over her shoulder and raised a questioning brow at him.

"Good morning, Gareth," she greeted him casually. "We'll be loading soon, after I've finished my coffee and the weather reports. I didn't expect to see you this early in the morning. Was there some problem I should know about?"

He regarded her narrowly for a long moment, and when he spoke, it was to ignore her opening gambit, pursuing his own train of thought.

"Good morning, Morgain. You're looking lovely this morning. Very . . . relaxed. I trust you had a restful night." His glance raked her, as though searching for signs of a disturbed sleep.

She smiled sunnily at him. "I had an excellent night, thank you. Should I not have?" she inquired innocently, and was secretly rewarded by his quickly erased scowl.

She sipped cautiously at her coffee and then gestured with the mug toward the pot. "Help yourself. You can use Ken's mug. It's the one with the green stripes. He won't be in for another hour."

She immersed herself in the reports again and stifled a snicker as she heard a muttered curse before he walked over to the pot and poured himself a cupful of the steaming, strong brew. She judged the time to a nicety and finished her own cup as he started to sit down across from her. She gathered the papers in her lap together, swung her legs down, and stood up.

"Time to earn my pay." She placed her mug on the tray by the coffeepot, tossed the reports on the counter, and pulled the orange from her shoulder bag, which she swung jauntily by the straps as she headed toward the door.

"I'll preflight the plane and supervise the loading. We'll be ready for takeoff in forty-five minutes."

She touched a finger to her forehead and went out the door, eyes sparkling with mischief. As she headed toward the waiting plane and men, she peeled the orange, tidily stowing the peel scraps in her bag to throw away later. The sections were tart and juicy, and she munched them with unalloyed enjoyment. She might not win many battles in this contest between herself and Gareth, but she would fully savor those she did.

When Gareth and John came toward her later, she was whistling under her breath as she lounged against the leading edge of the wing, watching their approach. As they neared she treated Gareth to another sunny smile before she turned her attention to John.

"All secured, John. I'll be back about eleven for the live load. I can grab a bite to eat while Bob converts the plane back to a passenger configuration, and we'll take off at 1300." She grinned impishly at him. "Maybe by then their lunches will have settled. I warn you, if one of them develops even the faintest tinge of green, I'll introduce him to the fine sport of sky diving. If I'm in a good mood, I might even loan him a parachute." She turned to Gareth. "Do you have some sunglasses with you? We'll be flying into the sun for a while and you'll need them."

He patted his shirt pocket and responded dryly, "I'm ready if you are, captain."

Morgain welcomed the weekend with the fervor of a prisoner looking forward to parole. She had flown into Buckeye every day since service had been inaugurated,

74

and though Gareth had not accompanied her after that first day's flight, she had had dinner with him each evening.

The resolve to continue to rebuff his advances was beginning to fray her nerves badly since she discovered that she was now fighting a battle on two fronts. Her own body was proving traitor. The insidious memory of his kisses and the touch of those lean-fingered hands plagued her, waking and sleeping, and the knowledge that she could experience them again, and more, anytime she desired was a torment more refined than she would ever have believed possible.

When she was with Gareth in the evenings, she maintained, successfully she devoutly hoped, an air of self-mocking enjoyment. She did not try to hide the fact that she was attracted to him. He was far too experienced not to know it, and she had given herself away by her response to his kisses and caress the night of their first dinner together.

She could not feign indifference to him. To try would be as revealing as total surrender, so she was left with the course of action she now employed. She went out with him whenever he asked her, but held him at arm's length through a carefully balanced attitude of reserve, amusement at herself and him, and avoidance of situations where his physical magnetism could overwhelm her defenses. When all else failed, she picked a fight with him.

The strain was tremendous. John and Ken felt the bite of her temper, and her mother and father watched with worried eyes when she prowled the house like a restless inmate testing the limits of his cell.

Saturday morning found Morgain, coffee cup in hand, surveying the lowering gray skies with grim disfavor from

75

the vantage point of the kitchen window. She had risen early, planning to escape the house with a picnic lunch. The thought of a day of solitude took on an extraordinarily attractive aspect. She knew if she stayed housebound, she would only manage to drive herself and her long-suffering parents up the proverbial wall. An even more cogent reason to absent herself was that if she didn't, she was morbidly certain that Gareth would annex her for the entire day, instead of just the evening she had already agreed to.

When the phone rang, she eyed it as she would have regarded a coiled and rattling snake. With a superstitious, irrational dread she was sure that she had managed to conjure him up by merely thinking his name. Seeing that she was not going to answer it, her mother rose from the kitchen table and lifted the receiver, cutting off the strident peal in midring. After a moment's low-voiced conversation her mother held out the phone with unmistakable intent.

"It's for you, dear." A smile, amused and aware, followed Morgain's undisguised look of dismay. "It's John."

"Oh."

Morgain gave her mother a shamefaced grin and took the phone.

"Hi, John. Morgain here."

"Glad you're up, Morgain. We've got problems."

Morgain felt a frisson of foreboding feather her spine. John was given more to understatement than hyperbole, and the husky, strained quality in his voice told her there was something seriously amiss. She had a sinking feeling that she was about to become personally involved in whatever had gone wrong.

He continued, "There's been an accident."

76

She felt a freezing clutch of fear. "Ken?" she gasped, and her parents, alerted by her face and tone of voice, looked up.

"No, no! Sorry, Morgain. I didn't mean to scare you." Morgain sighed and shook her head reassuringly at her mother and father. "Ken's fine," John continued. "There's been an accident at Buckeye. One of the construction workers managed to flip a 'cat' over on himself. I understand that he's in a pretty bad way."

Morgain's brain began to tick over as her professional instincts came to fore. While half of her brain listened to John, a portion began to consider which one of the aircraft would convert most quickly and efficiently into an air ambulance.

"Are you already at the field, John?" she asked crisply.

"Yes, I came down as soon as Gareth called me. Ken's on his way here too." He was equally crisp.

"What's the latest forecast for here and there?"

"The weather's bad and getting worse. It's above minimums right now, but that will probably change within the hour, for here. Buckeye has maybe an hour and a half extra before they sock in. I've been in contact with the doctor at Buckeye, and he says that the man is in no shape to be moved, even if the weather holds, so we can't air-evac him back."

"All right, John. Give me the rest."

"Okay. The man has a rare blood type and there are no donors of his type at Buckeye for a direct transfusion. The doctor says he needs surgery within the next few hours, as well as transfusions, but if we can bring in some blood and a field surgery pack he can do the operation there with a fair chance of success. If we can't, the man will die."

John paused to answer a question from someone in the

77

room with him. Morgain could hear him say, "I've got her on the phone now," before he came back on the line. He continued, "I've contacted the hospital and they're laying it on. A courier will have everything at the field within an hour."

"John, I'll be at the field in twenty minutes. Have Ken make up the survival pack. He knows what I'll want. Have the latest weather ready and preflight the plane for me. The sooner I get off, the better for all concerned."

"Now, Morgain, I haven't said you'll be flying—"

She cut him off ruthlessly. "John, you're wasting time. We both know why you called me and why I'm the one to go. No false modesty and no evasions. I'll see you in twenty minutes."

She hung up and headed for the door. "Accident at Buckeye. I have to make a mercy flight up there. Mom, fix a thermos of coffee, please. I've got to dress."

She ran into her bedroom and stripped off her houserobe and shortie gown, yanking out bra, briefs, and thermal underwear from a drawer as she dropped the nightclothes on the floor. Two pairs of heavy socks were pulled up over the legs of the thermals; then she pulled on heavy denim jeans and a sturdy denim work shirt. She rummaged in a drawer, muttering an imprecation when the belt she was searching for eluded her immediate grasp. When she finally located it beneath a pile of scarves, she threaded it through the belt loops on her jeans with a sigh of relief. It was formed of dark blue nylon, braided and knotted into a decorative and eye-catching design, but that was not why she chose it. It could be unbraided to form a length of nylon cord with a breaking strain of over 250 pounds. She had made it herself when she started camping as a teen-ager, and the belt had been made and unmade four times for various purposes. She hoped that she would not need it for a fifth time today.

In the back of her closet she located sturdy, well-worn hiking boots, and their laced support was comforting promise that whatever else she had to contend with, a broken ankle would not be one of her problems. From another drawer she lifted a finely honed hunting knife and slid it into the sheath designed for it in her boot. Two large, men's white handkerchiefs and a folded jackknife, the type with various tools hidden in its body as well as several sizes of blades, went into her jeans' pockets, and a waterproofed packet of matches was buttoned into a pocket of her shirt. These items and more would be duplicated in the survival pack that Ken would have ready for her, but if the worst happened and the plane went down, she could well become separated from the pack.

She had no illusions about what she was about to undertake. If the weather was at all above minimums, she would be taking off within the hour and her skill would be tested to its utmost limits. She knew her capabilities, and she wouldn't take off if the odds were against her. She was neither vainglorious nor foolhardy, but a man was dying and she would give him a chance for life if she could.

She braided her hair in one thick plait, securing it with a heavy rubber band. It gave her a childish look totally belied by the calm, grave planes of her face. She caught up a fleece-lined denim jacket and walked quickly to the kitchen. Her mother was waiting with the filled thermos of coffee, her face concerned, but trying to mask the fear that consumed her. Morgain was grateful as never before for her parents. They did not try to hold her back, having long ago accepted her as an adult capable of ordering her own life. They would wait in fear for word of her safety, but they would send her off with a kiss and a hug.

"Shall I drive you, chick?" was her father's only question.

"No, thanks, Dad. Stay here with Mom. You might give Jenny a call, though, and let her know that Ken won't be going. I don't want her to worry about him and I don't know if he'll remember to call her right away."

She kissed both of her parents and went swiftly out to the car. The drive to the airfield was quick, and she was pulling up in front of the office well within the twenty minutes she had allotted. She left the keys in the car. Someone would move it to the parking lot later.

The door opened and Gareth stood framed in the doorway. His gaze swept over her in one comprehensive look, and his face took on a thunderous glower.

"What the hell are you doing here?" he rasped out as he blocked her entry.

"Don't waste my time, Gareth," she snapped back. "This has nothing to do with you. I've got a lot to do and very little time. Move."

His jaw dropped. Here was no beautiful, sensuous woman but a hard-eyed professional intent on the job. She pushed past him with no more ado, and he turned to watch her stride over to John as he stood by the counter going over the latest weather reports. They went immediately into a low-voiced conference, and Gareth watched John shake his head in disagreement as Morgain emphasized a point. He finally came to reluctant acquiescence, and Gareth could contain himself no longer. He walked over and joined the group.

"Are you out of your mind, John? Morgain can't fly up to Buckeye in this weather. I forbid it."

Morgain didn't even glance up at him. John started to speak, but Morgain cut in even as his mouth opened.

"A man is dying, Gareth. He needs what I can bring him. The weather is still above minimums and I'll be taking off as soon as the courier arrives with the supplies."

"All right, but someone else can make the flight. I forbid *you* to go. John is under contract to Hammond Enterprises and I hold final authority on who flies the runs."

John opened his mouth again, and again Morgain forestalled him. This time she looked directly at Gareth, and her eyes were calm and determined. "There *is* no one else, Gareth. I'm the best one for the job. This isn't a contract flight. This is a mercy mission and you have no authority concerning who goes or stays." Her head lifted in a listening attitude. The wail of a police siren carried faintly through the air. She looked at John and nodded her head toward the door. "The courier is coming. Has Ken got the aircraft preflighted and my pack ready?"

"Yes," John replied heavily. "Morgain, are you sure . . . ?"

"Yes, John. You know it and I know it, so let's shelve the discussion." She turned to head for the door, and Gareth grabbed her arm.

"Just a minute. I may not be able to stop you, but I can go with you." His face was grim and tight.

Morgain smiled slightly. "Sorry again. You can't stop me and you can't go with me." She held up her hand to silence him. "It would serve no useful purpose to have you along, and your weight would just use up valuable fuel. You're not a doctor or a nurse, Gareth. I refuse to take you. Let's go, John."

They went out into the gusting wind and saw the police

car come to a sliding halt beside the waiting aircraft. Two men began unloading boxes, and Morgain hurried over to supervise the stowing and securing. As the final box was lashed in place Ken handed Morgain a loaded canvas bag. Gareth eyed it with suspicion.

"What's that?" he asked Morgain.

"Dirty laundry," she grinned at him.

"Morgain . . ."

"All right, nosey," she teased him. "They're some things Ken hopes I won't have to use." His expression grew more forbidding. "It's a survival pack. Now, are you happier knowing?" She put a hand on his arm, feeling with a sense of shock the rock-hard tenseness beneath the shirt. "Gareth, it's just a precaution. It doesn't mean— Oh, blast. I've got to go."

She tossed the pack onto the copilot's seat and turned to accept a kiss on the forehead and a hug from both Ken and John. She stood before Gareth for a moment, drinking in the sight of his face. He swept her into his arms and held her close against the hard length of his body, as though he would weld her to him. His kiss was keep and despairing, wrenched from the unconscious depths of unacknowledged feelings. He cupped her face with hard, warm palms and looked deeply into her eyes.

"Come back, Morgain. Please."

She touched the side of his face wonderingly and smiled at him. "I will, Gareth. I promise." She kissed his lips in a butterfly farewell and entered the plane.

They could see her stowing the canvas bag and beginning takeoff preparations. Ken removed the chocks from the wheels, and they moved back to safety as she began the engine run-up. She tossed them a farewell salute, and the plane began to taxi out to the runway for takeoff. The men stood in silent tension as the plane began its takeoff roll and rose smoothly into the air, making a climbing turn to orient itself for the flight to Buckeye. The drone of the engine was borne away by the whipping wind, and the three men waved good-bye to the courier and his police escort, after which they made their way back to the office. When they were inside, Ken excused himself.

"I want to call Mom and Dad and Jenny to let them know Morgain got off okay and that I'll be here until we hear from Buckeye."

He went into the inner office to make his phone calls, and Gareth turned to John, surveying him with unconcealed anger.

"All right, John. Let's have the truth. Just what are the chances?"

John didn't evade his eyes. "For me or for Ken, about 60-40."

Gareth paled visibly, and his eyes grew bleak. His fists clenched, and he took an involuntary half step toward the door. John hastened into speech.

"But for Morgain? Gareth, she's the best damn pilot I've ever seen. She's got reflexes like a mongoose and not a nerve in her body in an emergency. Believe me, if any human being can make this flight, she can."

Gareth's voice was bitter and tortured. "She's not just any human! You've let her fly off into probable death. If anything happens to her—"

"I didn't *let* her go, Gareth," John denied. "She chose to go. You don't know Morgain at all if you think anyone could have held her back. She's not a fool, and she's not bucking for the title of heroine. She knows her capabilities, and believe me, if she hadn't felt that she could see this flight through, she would have refused to go. She knows

83

it won't do this man who's injured any good if she ends up smashed into a mountain somewhere." Gareth flinched, and his mouth twisted in a hard slash.

John continued steadily, "When it comes to flying, Morgain is first and foremost a professional. I taught her and I know. At seventeen she was a better pilot than I ever hoped to be. She has an instinct for it and nothing interferes with her judgment when it comes to a question about flying. It's as though a switch snaps on somewhere inside of her, bypassing all her emotions and leaving only the critical and intellectual faculties functioning. I've seen it time and time again and it never ceases to amaze me. I don't know how she does it, and I suspect she doesn't know either. If I understood it, I could perhaps learn how to do it myself and I'd be five times as good a pilot as I am now. I can't stop your worrying about her. I'm worried about her myself, but she believes she can do it and therefore I believe she can do it. Now we just sweat it out. You pour the coffee"—he gestured toward the thermos of coffee that Morgain had brought from home, and Gareth closed his eyes in pain—"and I'll get on the radio to Buckeye to let them know she's on the way."

CHAPTER IV

Forever after, Morgain never spoke of the flight she made that day. When John asked for technical details, she turned his questions aside, commenting that she had been too busy to take notes, but added that if he wanted to write a letter to Cessna to let them know that their listed stress tolerances for the aircraft were underestimated, she would sign it. That was all he could get out of her, question as he would.

When Morgain finally taxied to a stop on the runway at Buckeye, her arms were shaky with fatigue and her wrists ached with a burning band of pain that encircled each wrist like red-hot manacles. She wearily released the seat harness that had saved her from being thrown about in the cockpit like a dried pea in its shell, and opened the door to the men who clustered about the plane, ready to receive her precious cargo.

A big, burly man she recognized as the construction foreman lifted her down from the plane, and others began to unload the plane like busy ants, jogtrotting their burdens toward the infirmary with careful speed. She stood watching them, too weary for the moment to move out of the whipping wind and spitting rain.

Finally she looked up at the foreman and asked, "How is your man?"

"He's hanging on," he reassured her. "The doctor is ready to start transfusing him, and by the time Dick has had some blood, they'll be set up and ready to start the operation. Doc Jenkins has a nurse and a guy who was a medic in the army to assist him, and we set up and scrubbed down a makeshift operating room under the doc's direction while you were on your way here."

"He doesn't need me to assist, then? I have had advanced first-aid training and I'm not squeamish, but to tell you the truth, if I don't have a cup of coffee soon I won't be fit to tie my own shoelaces." She smiled wearily up at the man beside her.

"I'm a prize idiot!" he expostulated. "You're worn out and here we are standing out in the rain."

He hustled her toward the cafeteria with ground-devouring strides. With great dispatch he ushered her into the warmly lit room and bellowed for coffee. The cook brought Morgain a hot, fragrant mug and, with a wink, liberally laced it with brandy. While she was sipping it the foreman disappeared and returned with a big towel that she gratefully accepted, using it to mop the moisture from her face and arms.

"Thanks," she smiled up at him in gratitude.

"No," he replied seriously. "The thanks are all due from us. We all know what you risked to bring the supplies and blood here for Dick, and if there's ever anything any of us can do for you, you only have to ask."

Morgain smiled again in reply and took another sip of the coffee. As its warmth and alcoholic heat pierced the mist of fatigue, she looked at the foreman in sudden inquiry. "Did anyone notify John that I arrived in one piece? They'll be climbing the walls by now."

Chagrin flooded the foreman's face. "Good lord, we forgot. In all the excitement it slipped my mind. Gareth will skin me with a dull knife. He's been checking with us every fifteen minutes since you took off."

He hurried out without another word, and Morgain leaned back in her chair and laughed weakly. The foreman was a veritable giant, but the dismay when he mentioned his probable fate at Gareth's hands was all too real. She had no doubt that the foreman was in for an uncomfortable roasting from Gareth for his tardy report of her arrival.

Her surmise was proved all too correct, judging from the expression worn by the hapless foreman when he returned some time later. Morgain had finished her coffee and was augmenting her body warmth by ingesting some of the excellent homemade vegetable soup brought to her by the hovering cook. He almost sidled around the door, and Morgain fancied she could still see traces of red around his ears. He gave her a sheepish grin and sat down in the chair across the table from her.

"There was a lot of static, but Gareth managed to get his message across anyway." He seemed to pause in reminiscence of the words so recently spoken to him, a wry grimace twisting his face. "But at least they know you're here okay and they'll notify your family. Gareth gave me a message for you, too. He said he had talked to John about the risk factor involved in this flight and you and he were overdue for a talk when you got back."

Morgain flushed slightly, and her mouth tightened in an annoyed line. John must have shot off his mouth about the amount of peril involved in this flight, and now Gareth

87

was really on the warpath. When she got back to the airfield, John would hear a few choice words from her concerning the advisability of keeping one's mouth shut about certain subjects no matter who did the asking. Now all she needed was for Ken to let the same information slip to her parents and she'd never hear the end of it. *Men,* she castigated silently. *Blabbermouths every one.*

The rain was coming down in earnest now, gray, depressing sheets of it, and Morgain felt an overwhelming desire to crawl into a soft bed and let her bruised and aching body sink into the restoring oblivion of sleep. She wouldn't be flying home before tomorrow at the earliest, and before she went anywhere in that plane, she'd have to go over it from nose to tail tip and wing to wing. It had taken quite a twisting, and she rather suspected that it might need some structural repair before she'd trust it in the air again, at least while *she* was going to be aboard it!

She rose stiffly from the chair, masking a grimace at the discomfort the movement cost her. The brandy in the coffee was making her somewhat light-headed, and a swimming sense of fatigue shadowed her face. She pushed the hair back off her forehead and turned to the foreman.

"Is there a place where I can get a hot shower and commandeer a bed for a few hours' sleep, Mr. . . . ?" She let her question trail off as she suddenly realized that she didn't know the foreman's name.

"Charley Vance," he hastily supplied. "Call me Charley. Of course we'll find you a bed and a shower. Come on and I'll take you to the dormitory block."

"Thanks, Charley. I'm Morgain." She gave him a warm, sleepy smile and followed him gratefully out the door. They jogtrotted through the rain to another building and he led her to a small suite of rooms consisting of living room, bedroom, and bath, obviously as yet unoccupied. Someone, however, had made the bed with fresh sheets. Clean towels were piled on the counter in the bathroom, flanked by new cakes of soap, a tube of toothpaste, and a cellophane wrapped toothbrush.

"Is there anything else you need that we can get for you, Morgain?" Charley queried her anxiously. "You've only to ask and if we've got it, I'll get it for you."

"Thanks Charley, but all I need now is a bath and a nap. Have you heard anything about Dick?"

"They started the operation about twenty minutes ago, but we won't know anything more for several hours." He paused and then continued, "Well, if there's nothing else . . ."

At the shake of her head he lifted a hand in farewell and went out, closing the door firmly behind him. Morgain stood for a moment, shoulders slumped in fatigue, and then retraced her steps to the bedroom. She began to peel off her jacket, not hiding the grimace the effort pulled from her, since there was no one to see. The jacket was damp, and she hoped that the someone who had made up the bed and supplied the towels had also remembered some coat hangers.

The bedroom closet yielded an ample supply, and she hung up the jacket, her shirt, jeans, and thermal leggings as she removed each item. Her boots went in the closet. She rinsed out one pair of socks and her underwear in the handbasin and draped them over heater vents to dry. The underwear, being nylon, would dry almost immediately, and the socks would be dry by tomorrow. She would wear the other pair.

She walked naked into the bathroom and caught sight of herself in the bathroom mirror. She surveyed without surprise the rapidly darkening bruises crisscrossing her shoulders. She had suspected they might be showing up soon and that they'd blossom in full glory during the steaming hot bath she planned to soak in. They would certainly limit her wardrobe for a while, she mused. She could imagine what her parents would say if they saw them, let alone Gareth!

With a chuckle at his probable reaction should he ever discover the harness marks, she turned the taps on full force. Just as well he'd never get the chance. He was mad enough, thanks to John's indiscretions about the danger inherent in the flight. If he saw the bruises where she had been thrown against the harness straps as the plane was tossed around the sky by the down- and updrafts . . . well . . . She shuddered slightly.

The tub was comfortably full, and she turned off the taps with a twist of the wrist. She stepped gingerly into the tub, her breath indrawn with a gulp as the heat of the water penetrated her skin. As she sank deeper into the water the gasp became a sigh of pleasure and her face flushed from the rushing warmth of the water. Whoever designed this tub must have liked to soak, because the back sloped at a comfortable angle. She rested her neck and head against it, shoulders below the level of the water to obtain the full benefit of the hot water. Periodically she turned the hot-water tap on with her toes, sending a fresh surge of warmth into the bath.

Finally she noticed that her toes were beginning to resemble little wrinkled prunes, and she realized that she was going to have to get out of the enervating warmth and dry off. She flipped the drain switch up with her foot and, as the water began to gurgle out of the tub, rose with a groan to wrap herself in a voluminous towel.

She had been right, she thought gloomily. The hot water had indeed brought out the bruises nicely. No bikinis or low-cut tops for you, my girl, not for some time to come. Warm and dry at last, she brushed her teeth with the thoughtfully provided paste and toothbrush and, after neatly hanging up the damp towel, reentered the bedroom.

The turned-back sheets were cool to her heated skin, and she stretched and wiggled in voluptuous abandon. Then with a muttered curse she got out of bed, stomped over to the wall, and flicked off the light switch. The bed felt even better the second time she slid into it, and she turned on her side with a sigh and was instantly asleep.

Waking was gradual and pleasant, until she injudiciously moved her shoulders. For a moment disorientation after sleep puzzled her as to the cause behind her discomfort, but memory returned all too swiftly and for a long instant she was caught in the web of painful recall of that flight. Shuddering, she came back to the present and the reality of the night-shadowed room and rumpled sheets beneath her naked body.

Fully awake at last, Morgain reached out for her watch, but the darkness defeated her. She groped her way across the room to where she hoped she remembered the light controls and swept her hand over the textured wall until she encountered the switch, flicking it upward to flood the room with eye-squinting light. The room was chill, coming from the warm cocoon of the sheet and blankets, and goose pimples roughened her skin. Hastily Morgain donned her underclothes and buttoned her heavy shirt over her shrinking flesh. She pulled on the now dried jeans and tugged the socks on toes that had returned to their normal unwrinkled state. When warmth had subdued the goose pimples, she went into the bathroom and splashed her face with cool water to banish the last remnants of sleep still drugging her brain. Her hair was still held firmly in its confining pigtail, but was sadly wispy. She unplaited it and ran the small comb, which she had been foresighted enough to stick into her jeans pocket, through the heavy strands, disciplining them to silken order again.

Vanity had not extended to bringing makeup and lipstick along, but on the whole she was not dissatisfied with her appearance. Her body felt as though someone had been beating her with a large and well-wielded stick, but no sign of the generalized ache appeared on her face. She did shift the straps of her bra slightly so that they were not pressing on the sorest areas of her shoulders, but only time and a healthy constitution would mend the rest.

Morgain assumed that she would be spending the night in this room, so she decided to leave her jacket and extra socks, which were still damp, where they were, to dry out completely. As she was pulling on her boots she regarded the hunting knife in its sheath and debated whether to leave it in the room too, but decided that she might as well leave it alone. It would be hidden by her jeans anyway.

When Morgain entered the cafeteria again she was surrounded by a large group, all eager to congratulate her on her feat and hear the precise details. She fended off their questions with aplomb and turned the conversation into other channels by asking after the man on whose behalf she had made the flight. Charley had pushed his way through the throng, and it was to him she rather desperately addressed her questions.

"Charley, how's Dick? Was the operation a success?"

"Lay off, you lot!" Charley thundered at the engulfing mob, and they reluctantly dispersed somewhat. He turned back to Morgain, who gave him an impish but grateful smile. "The doc finished up some time ago," Charley continued, answering her original question, "and he says Dick's holding his own. He won't commit himself, but we all know that before and without surgery Dick had no chance at all, so 'holding his own' is better than nothing."

Morgain sipped thoughtfully at her coffee, which the cook had again laced with brandy, though with a lighter hand, she was glad to note. In a general way she was not adverse to alcohol in moderation, but continual dosing with brandy-laced coffee could leave her disgusted with both liquids.

The next morning she awoke early to bright blue skies, freshly laundered by yesterday's storm. She had managed to contact John late in the afternoon, in spite of the static, and had informed him that she wasn't going to return to the airfield until she had given the plane a thorough going-over the next day, so not to expect her until he saw her. The evening had been spent in convivial company, made more so by the news that Dick, the injured man, would recover and, almost miraculously, do so without permanent disability.

Morgain dressed swiftly, by now heartily sick of her limited wardrobe, and made her way into the cafeteria for breakfast. When the cook presented her with a cup of coffee as she came in the door, she sniffed it suspiciously, much to his amusement. She grinned amiably at him and carried it to the table where Charley and several of her more attentive escorts from the evening before were gesturing imperatively. As she slid into the chair Charley held out for her, he gave her a beaming grin.

"Dick's awake and he'd like to see you after breakfast. The doc says okay, and that you'd be the best medicine he could prescribe for him. I'll take you over later, if that's all right with you?"

"Of course, Charley. I'd like very much to meet Dick, if Dr. Jenkins doesn't think it'll tire him too much— Good Lord!" She broke off as the cook presented her with a plate positively piled high with succulent slices of ham, golden yellow scrambled eggs, and a pyramid of fluffy biscuits with melted butter oozing down the sides. "Thank you, it all looks delicious," she assured the hovering man with a smile. He went back to his duties beaming.

"Charley," she muttered, "help me out. I'll never get around all of this and if I did, I wouldn't fit in the plane, but I don't want to hurt his feelings." With a surreptitious glance over her shoulder she rapidly transferred half the contents of her plate onto Charley's, and at his remonstrance that he had already eaten and was full, she retorted, "You owe me. What was it you said, that if I needed anything I had only to ask? Well, I'm calling in the debt. I need help."

That sparked delighted laughter among the men, and it was this happy group that met Gareth and John's gaze when they came into the room. Gareth found himself prey to a coil of conflicting sensations: blindingly happy to see for himself that Morgain was indeed unharmed, furious with her for ever taking such a chance, and blackly jealous to find her the center of a circle of doting admirers.

It was the latter emotion that jolted him to a stop inside the doorway, leaving John to continue toward the group unaware. In his whole life, Gareth had never been jealous of a woman's attraction for other men. He realized with painful honesty that he had never been jealous because he had never cared anything for the previous women in his life except as they represented amusement or sometimes

94

temporary sexual gratification. He was no libertine, but neither was he a monk, and there had been women.

He had thought to make Morgain one of them. From the moment she had faced him in the hangar, with a smear of grease on her cheek, he had desired her and had promised himself he'd have her. Since then she had rocked him back on his heels so many times that he had lost count. She had the face of an angel and the aroused temper of a rabid ermine. The thought of taming her put an itch in the palm of his hand and an extra degree of temperature in the blood racing through his body. He was frequently seized with an almost overwhelming desire to spank or possibly even strangle her, balanced by an even stronger yearning to stroke and fondle her, to make her purr for him.

At this interesting juncture of his thoughts Morgain looked up and saw the two men, John rapidly bearing down on her and Gareth standing by the outer door glowering at her, mayhem and murder burning deep in his eyes.

Her reaction was typical. She jumped up and rushed into John's bear hug, and as he crushed her to him she murmured in his ear, "You have a big mouth, my very dear friend. Whatever on God's green earth possessed you to tell Gareth how dangerous the flight was? It was none of his damn business, and I'll thank you to keep a still tongue about things like that from now on." She gave him a fond kiss on the cheek and an angelic smile. John sensibly made no reply to her speech. He knew her very well indeed.

By this time Gareth was approaching the tender scene, and Morgain favored him with an angelic smile too. It had no visible effect on his scowl. Morgain's own temper began to kindle, but with heroic self-control she tried to avert the inevitable—she was afraid—explosion.

She turned her attention back to John and with reasonable surprise said, "John, I'm surprised to see you and Gareth here; I didn't know there was a consignment scheduled to come up here on Sunday."

John's face was rapidly assuming the dusky hue of embarrassment, and he offered tentatively, "Well, actually we didn't bring a load. Gareth felt . . . that is, we thought . . ." He floundered and then got it out in a rush. "I brought Jack up with us to go over the plane, to be sure it's airworthy before we take it back home. You know, Jack being our mechanic and all. . . ."

I know Jack is our mechanic and all, John," Morgain agreed in the most saccharin of tones. John paled. "What I didn't realize was that you had suddenly come to the conclusion that I am no longer competent to recognize when an aircraft is no longer airworthy. Granted, there are some jobs . . . I detest welding, for instance . . . that Jack does *ever* so much better than I do"—her voice was getting progressively softer and sweeter, a feat in itself since her teeth were clenched—"but that does not make me incapable of deciding whether a plane is airworthy and if it is not, whether the repair of said aircraft is beyond my meager skills." The final words of this statement were delivered in an evenly spaced monotone. Her voice was quiet, but her look was fulminating.

John had a thin film of perspiration beading his forehead, and the collar of his open-necked shirt gave the impression of being suddenly far too tight. Morgain surveyed him with something akin to loathing, but when she looked at Gareth it was no longer merely akin, it *was* loathing.

She addressed herself to the empty space between the two men. "I think I'll go out and watch Jack work. Maybe he'll let me hand him a screwdriver now and then, after, of course, he shows me what a screwdriver looks like." She left.

All the men in the room released a collective breath. John and Gareth exchanged what is generally called a speaking look, and John shook his head ruefully.

"I told you she wouldn't be pleased. I haven't seen her in such a temper since a visiting Italian pilot pinched her on the bottom and offered to take her for a ride in a real airplane. She took him up in a borrowed crop duster and brought him down a delicate shade of pea green." He shivered. "God knows what she'll do to me."

"Don't worry. I'll take care of it," Gareth reassured John with the confidence born of ignorance.

"It's kind of you to offer to sacrifice yourself to save me. 'Greater love hath no man . . .' and all that, but I don't think she'll actually murder me. Deep down she's really awfully fond of me, and she'll remember that in a year or so. Of course, the interim may be rather sticky . . ." John sighed and then brightened. "Maybe Ken can talk to her. She listens to him . . . sometimes."

"I said I'll talk to her," Gareth stated firmly. "What that young woman needs is to be turned over someone's knee and paddled."

With that pungent observation he strode out of the room in search of Morgain. John stared at the closed door for a long moment and shook his head. "What I wouldn't give to be a fly on the wall when he catches up with her," he commented to Charley, who had come to stand beside him. He chuckled and continued, "Of course we'll quite probably be able to hear them both all the way in here. Got

97

any really strong black coffee around the place? I sure could use a cup."

Morgain had not gone out to watch Jack. Instead she went first to the room she had occupied the night before, intending to collect her jacket and dry socks. Once she had them she would go out to the plane. She and Jack, working together, could check the plane over double-quick, and, luck being with her, there would be nothing major amiss. If that proved to be the case, she would shake the dust of Buckeye from her feet, break a few speed records back to home base, and go to her parents' house. Once there she would pack her bags and leave John and Gareth Hammond to stew in their own juices. She ground her teeth together.

With this most satisfying course of action laid out, she went into the bedroom and pulled her jacket off the hanger. She collected the extra socks and rolled them into a ball, which she stuffed in the pocket of the jacket. With the jacket slung over her shoulder she headed toward the door. She had almost reached it when it was thrown violently open, to rebound against the wall with a mighty crash.

Framed in the doorway was six feet plus of black-browed man with glittering green eyes. Hands on hips he advanced into the room, forcing her to retreat several steps or be run down. Gareth shut the door behind him with ostentatious gentleness and faced her again.

"So this is where you're sulking," he began.

Morgain's breath hissed through her clenched teeth, and in accents of purest vitrol she answered, "I am not sulking. I came here to pick up my jacket and now I'm going out to the plane."

"No, you're not. I have something to say to you. First

of all, it was my idea to bring Jack up here to check over the plane, not John's."

"I know that," she snarled. "John knows better. He knows that I would have radioed him after checking the plane if I'd found anything wrong that I couldn't fix myself or hadn't the tools to handle. It might not have been necessary for Jack to fly up here at all."

She started to go around him to get to the door. To prevent this Gareth's hands shot out and grasped her gently by the shoulders. He exerted very little of the considerable strength he possessed, merely desiring to prevent Morgain from leaving the room precipitately before he was finished talking, but unfortunately his large hands came down squarely on top of the worst of the bruises the harness straps had inflicted on Morgain's shoulders. She flinched, yelped involuntarily, and jerked away from his touch.

"What the hell—" Gareth looked at her in astonishment.

Morgain reddened and met his eyes defiantly. Gareth's eyes narrowed in speculation and then widened in dawning comprehension. He took a step toward her and Morgain backed up, hand half lifted to fend him off.

"Let me see your shoulders, Morgain," Gareth commanded her softly.

"No." She took another step backward.

"Now, Morgain, we can do this easy or hard," he informed her, "but I am going to look at your shoulders." He advanced another step.

Morgain looked around like a trapped animal. He was still between her and the door, but if she could lure him far enough away from it, and if she was fast enough

. . . She backed slowly and steadily away from him. He followed a step at a time.

"My shoulders are none of your business, Gareth." As she spoke he took another step toward her. She exploded into action. She feinted to the left, threw her jacket at his head, and took off running like a scalded cat to his right, heading toward the door.

Suddenly an iron-muscled arm caught her around the waist and yanked her back into a rock-hard chest, forcing the breath from her lungs in an agonized "Whoof!" While she was still gasping for air she was swept up high against him, carried into the bedroom, and ignominiously dumped on the bed. Gareth knelt beside her, grasped her wrists, and pulled her arms back to pin them beneath her body. She managed to fill her straining lungs and started to struggle, kicking her legs and writhing in fury.

"Lie still, you little idiot. I don't want to hurt you. I just want to look at your shoulders," Gareth panted as he sought to contain her bucking, lunging figure beneath his heavier body.

Now beside herself with rage, Morgain didn't waste any precious breath answering him. She just redoubled her efforts to kick him and/or get loose. Gareth realized that she would manage to do both if he didn't move quickly, and he reacted instinctively. He pinned the lower half of Morgan's thrashing body down with his and slid his free hand around the nape of her neck to twine in her hair, immobilizing her head.

"Now lie *still*, you hellion!" he ordered sternly.

Morgain gave one final convulsive heave and subsided, giving Gareth the proverbial look that could kill. As she lay glaring up at him he warily removed his hand from her head and deliberately undid the top buttons of her shirt.

With infinite care Gareth shifted his lower body slightly, cautiously easing away from her enough to allow him to pull her shirt out of the waistband of her jeans, while not allowing her the opportunity to kick him with any force should she be so inclined, which she was.

That much accomplished, he drew a deep breath and pulled up and out on the shirt at the neck, baring first one shoulder and then the other. His face was expressionless as he looked down at the wicked, dark bruises that ran in broad strips from the tops of her shoulders down onto skin still covered by the shirt, but a pulse began to throb at his left temple.

Without a word he rolled off of her, releasing her, and lay beside her on the bed, staring up at the ceiling. Morgain pulled her arms out from under her body, relieving the strain on her back and shoulders, but made no other move for a long minute. Then she wearily rebuttoned her shirt, sat up, and swung her legs over the edge of the bed.

"You could have been killed." His voice was low and full of some strong emotion . . . pain or anger . . . she couldn't tell which.

"Yes." Her reply was flat, acknowledgment and acceptance of the truth of his statement. "John or Ken would have been." There was no pride or boast inherent in those words. She said it as a fact. "That's why I went and they didn't. I am here. Neither of them would have been."

"But you might not have been here either."

Now she recognized the emotion. It was anger.

"I have said it," she reiterated her agreement, "but I *am* here and Dick is alive. I would do the same again."

Suddenly she was jerked back flat on the bed and Gareth was once again over her, pressing her down into the softness of the bed with the weight of his lean, hard body. She saw a hot glitter of green eyes and then all sight was blotted out as his lips ravaged her mouth. It was punishment and passion, torment and transport. Under the dominance of his savage masculinity she lay pliant and yielding, exhausted by past rage and present rapture. Without taking her body, he nonetheless possessed her mind, branding her with the scent and feel and taste of himself, a rape of the senses.

Then, as suddenly as he had begun his assault on her senses, he stopped. He lifted his head and looked at her face, a bitter twist to the lips that so recently had ravaged the intimate secrets of her mouth.

"Damn you, Morgain. You tear a man's soul out of his body."

Before she could move, before she could say a word, he was gone. She heard the door slam behind him, and a cold chill replaced the heat of his body's passion.

She didn't know how long she lay on the bed, but at last she rose, tucked her shirt back into the waistband of her jeans, and went into the living room. Stiffly she bent over and picked up her jacket from the floor, tucked it under her arm, and left the room.

She went by the infirmary on her way to the plane, but was thankful to be told that the patient was asleep. She left a message of good wishes and promised to stop by the next time she came into Buckeye. Her mental "if ever" was heard by no one but herself.

Jack was finishing his inspection of the plane as she approached. His cheerful "Morgain, you've got the luck of the devil" was no particular balm to her spirit. She made some indeterminate sound in her throat and opened the cockpit door to toss her coat inside on the seat.

"Cessna builds good planes." She pushed the hair up off

the back of her neck and tried to massage the tension out of her nape. "What's the damage?"

"A few loose nuts and bolts and some dents that we can take care of back at the base. Did you run into some hail?"

Her laugh was thin. "Jack, I ran into everything. Well, let's get down to it. I want to get this crate back to base. Seems as though I've been a long time gone."

They worked in well-practiced partnership for an hour, and at last Morgain downed tools and began cleaning her hands. Jack stowed the rest of the tools, and she silently handed him a rag and tube of grease cleanser.

"Want to ride home with me?" she offered. "I don't know when John's leaving, but I'll be taking off as soon as I've said good-bye to Charley."

"Thanks. Maybe I can still salvage some of my Sunday. I was supposed to take the family on a picnic today."

Morgain's face was impassive, but she only said, "In that case I'll have you home before noon. I'll make my adieux now. Be right back."

She found Charley in the cafeteria, although most of the other men had dispersed. He and John and Gareth were deep in conversation, which cut off abruptly when Morgain entered the room. She crossed to the group with easy, fluid grace, the ravages of the past day showing not at all on her serene countenance. The men all stood up as she neared. She smiled up at Charley with warmth, holding out her hand.

"I'm leaving now, Charley, but I wanted to say good-bye and thanks for the hospitality. Tell the rest of the men good-bye for me, please."

When Charley released her hand, she slanted a look at John. "Jack is going back with me. He's overdue at a picnic and I promised to have him home by noon." A smile for Charley and a frosty "Gentlemen," and she turned away. There was no look or word for Gareth, but she was aware of his dark presence with every fiber of her being. She kept an even, unhurried pace to the door and exited without a backward look.

Morgain walked out to the waiting plane feeling as old as death. Jack was already strapped in, waiting for her. She climbed in beside him and said briefly, "All set. I told John we were leaving."

The flight home was silent for the most part. Jack sensed that Morgain was not in the mood for light chatter, and his only vocal contribution was his attempt to find out if she blamed him for the events that had brought him up to check over her plane.

"Uh, Morgain. You know it wasn't my idea to come up here and go over the plane. John called me at home last night and told me we were coming to Buckeye this morning at first light."

"It's all right, Jack. I know very well whose idea it was to drag you up here. I'm not mad at you."

And that was the sum total of conversation for the flight. Morgain landed the plane smoothly, taxied it into the hangar where Jack could work on it Monday morning, and shut down the engine. With swift, economical motions she released herself from the harness and slid from the seat. If her closing of the door was a little more emphatic than usual (she slammed it hard enough to make Jack wince), Jack was a long-married man and far too canny in the ways of a woman in a temper to comment.

They walked together toward the parking lot, and Jack offered, "I don't see your car, Morgain. Can I drop you off on my way home?"

104

"Thanks, Jack. Someone must have collected it yesterday. I'd appreciate a ride home."

As they drew up in front of her parents' home, the front door opened and her mother and father stood framed in the doorway. Morgain got out of the car and thanked Jack for the ride, sending him off with a smile and a wave. She walked into her parents' warm embrace, and when she saw the tears sparkling on her mother's lashes she knew with a sinking heart that Ken had been as indiscreet as John. She could only hope that he had at least waited until news of her safe arrival had come in before burdening her parents with knowledge she would have given much to have spared them.

"Oh, Morgain," her mother cried as she clutched her daughter close. "Thank God you're all right. When we learned how dangerous the flight really was . . ."

Her father was less articulate, but she read the same concern in the strength of the hug he gave her. Her irritation with Ken was rapidly escalating into outright disgust. There had been no need to inflict his own worries on their parents. He'd probably managed to throw Jenny into a flat spin too! Her fixed intention to have A WORD with her brother became more urgent every minute.

As they all went into the house she attempted to smooth things over a little. "Now, really, it wasn't *that* bad! You both know me well enough to know that I wouldn't have gone if I hadn't felt the odds were in my favor. I'm no gambler, and you know I don't even like to lose money in the penny slots. Please, don't feel so bad. I'm fine and back in one piece and the man who was hurt is going to be all right." She continued rather desperately, "I'm so sorry you've had this extra worry. Ken had no business scaring you like that. I hope he had the decency to at least wait until you knew I was at Buckeye and all right," she finished bitterly.

By this time they had reached the kitchen, and her mother began automatically to pour cups of coffee. Morgain perched on the edge of the kitchen table, swinging one booted foot. Her mother handed her a cup, and Morgain dumped in sugar and milk, stirring it down with abstracted violence. She was mentally rehearsing what she was going to say to her overly articulate sibling.

Her mother swung toward her in surprise. "You mean Ken knew how dangerous it was and he let you go?" Suddenly some latent remnant of Grandfather Ryan's temper manifested itself, and Miri Kendrick proved that blood runs true. "Just wait until I get my hands on that big ox of a son!" she exploded. I haven't taken a hairbrush to him in twenty years, but when I get through with him he'll wish—"

"Whoa, whoa!" Morgain held up her hand in perplexity. She looked from one parent to the other in some bewilderment. Her father was regarding her mother with admiration.

He grinned and said, "Haven't seen you lose your temper like that in years, Miri love. Have I told you lately that you're beautiful when you're angry?"

The tension snapped and Miri laughed, her flash of temper dissipated by her husband's disarming words. "Not since the last time I lost my temper, Daniel. Maybe I should do it more often. A woman always likes to get a sincere compliment."

When the laughter had died down, Morgain doggedly returned to the subject. "Am I to gather that it *wasn't* from Ken that you learned about the risks involved in this flight?" She held up a hand as her mother opened her mouth. "And I promise you, Mom, it really wasn't as bad as you've evidently been led to believe. I swear to you that I wouldn't have gone if I hadn't been sure I could do it. It's true neither Ken nor John could have done it, just like I told Gareth . . ."

Her words trailed away and her eyes slitted in comprehension. She carefully placed her mug on the table and stilled her idly swinging leg. She looked from her mother to her father and knew she was correct. "I might have known it!" she all but shouted. "What ever gave that man the idea that he has the right to interfere in my life. . . . Well, this time he's gone too far! How *dare* he come here, behind my back, and meddle with things that don't concern him in the slightest—"

She stopped abruptly and took a deep breath. Her fists clenched once, twice, and then she mastered her outward signs of fury. Only the pinched whiteness about her nostrils and the compression of her lips into a thin line, so at variance with their normal soft fullness, betrayed her inward seething.

"Sorry. I didn't mean to take it out on you all," she apologized briefly to her stunned parents. "I'll reserve my fire for the one who deserves it." In a quiet voice that shook only slightly, she continued speaking in an unnaturally level tone.

"Please tell me exactly what happened. I gather Gareth came to see you after I took off." She sank back on the table edge and picked up her cooling coffee cup, to sip slowly from it and regard her uncomfortable parents over the rim.

She didn't miss the look that passed between her parents. She had often witnessed their almost telepathic communication and knew they were deciding which one of

107

them would be able to handle the telling most tactfully and soothingly. An unwilling grin tugged at the corners of her mouth, and she made a mental wager with herself, which she promptly won at her mother's infinitesimal nod of agreement toward her father. He cleared his throat and visibly marshaled his thoughts.

"Well, yes. Gareth did come to see us yesterday, Morgain. He came to tell us in person that you were at Buckeye and all right. It was very thoughtful of him," he added pacifically.

Morgain snorted but made no comment, waiting for him to continue.

He cleared his throat again and chose his words carefully. "You mustn't blame Gareth, my dear. He was . . . ah . . . upset when he got here. He'd been through a trying time and he was very worried about you."

Daniel thought this was a masterful description of the mood Gareth had been in when he had arrived at their front door. He had looked like a man who had come safely, but not unscathed, through the torments of hell, and it had been both Daniel's and Miri's opinion that the relief Gareth felt over Morgain's safe arrival at Buckeye had not yet had a chance to outweigh the long agony he had endured while awaiting news of the outcome of her desperate flight.

In Daniel's shrewd assessment of the man, Gareth was used to having complete control of events around him. The sudden realization that Morgain obstinately denied him any say-so about her decision to make the flight, coupled with her undoubted peril, had shaken him far out of his normal self-command. Gareth was not accustomed to having his decisions opposed and, even worse, overridden by a chit of a girl, especially one he had more than a passing interest in.

Daniel was a father, but he was also a man. He had noted with interest and some private amusement the way Gareth had looked at Morgain whenever he came to pick her up for dinner. Had not the undoubted desire he saw in the man's eyes been strongly tempered by wonder and a lurking tenderness, Daniel might have been goaded into the unwelcome and most probably futile role of heavy father.

"If you wish to assign blame, remember that your mother is very persuasive and uncomfortably intuitive." He chuckled slightly and added, "It's made it very difficult for me ever to deceive her during our married life."

"Why, Daniel," Miri interjected blandly, "I didn't know you'd ever tried to deceive me. How naughty of you. Was it about anything important?"

"Help! See what you got me into, Morgain, my dear?" He gave her a rueful glance and was glad to note that the tense whiteness had faded from around her nostrils and her lips were regaining their soft outlines. He hoped that Gareth would someday appreciate his efforts on his behalf. If he, Daniel, didn't succeed in defusing Morgain's temper before she next ran across Gareth, the man might never know what hit him. Well, he grinned inwardly, thirty years with Miri had more than adequately trained him in techniques suitable for handling the explosive Ryan females. Perhaps Gareth might like a tip or two. They might save him a couple of scars.

"Anyway," he continued smoothly, "Gareth came by to tell us that you had arrived and would be staying the night and that he and John would fly up at first light with Jack." He was treading on dangerous ground again. He could tell by the flare of her nostrils, and he delicately picked his way through the minefield. "Gareth felt that you . . . er . . . might have had a very rough flight and might not feel up to making the necessary repairs on the plane, so he asked John to bring Jack along to save you having to do the work yourself."

Morgain muttered, "In a pig's eye!"

Daniel wondered whether to let this pass or pursue it, but decided that belaboring the point might do more damage, so he pressed on. "When Gareth expressed his fears about the roughness of your flight, your mother picked up on it at once and wouldn't let the poor man rest until she had wrung every last scrap of information out of him. He was most unwilling, but your mother is relentless and she finally cornered him."

Suddenly Morgain burst into delighted laughter. She had just conjured up a vision of a tailed and whiskered Gareth being pounced upon by a tabby with the face of her mother. The whole image was too absurd to sustain for long, for Gareth was by no stretch of the imagination a "Wee, sleekit, cow'rin, tim'rous beastie."

Morgain lifted her coffee cup and saluted her mother mockingly. "The Grand Inquisitor. Did you have to resort to the rack, or were thumbscrews sufficient?"

Daniel relaxed back in his chair. The worst was over. His premature self-congratulations were cut off in midflow when Morgain continued.

"Too bad I don't believe it. Gareth Hammond never gave away any information he didn't want to, and he had a purpose in telling you what he did, no matter how 'unwilling' he seemed to be. Shall I lay out the scenario for you? I'm sure he was worried . . . after all, he does have the overall responsibility for Buckeye, and if something

110

had happened to me on this flight"—she saw her mother flinch—"sorry, Mom, but it's done and over with now. Anyway, as I said, he feels primary responsibility for Buckeye and whatever concerns it. He's the man in charge. Too, I'm a woman and therefore to be protected from the rough side of life. The mere thought that I'm out there laying my life on the line is enough to raise every male chauvinist hackle he has, and believe me, he's got plenty of them."

Morgain walked over to the coffeepot and replenished her cup, stirring in sugar and milk with thoughtful strokes. "Gareth Hammond considers women to be decorative icing on the cake, sweet but with no real substance. The idea that anyone, but more especially a *mere woman,* should defy his authority is enough to really jolt him, and I did it in an unfortunately flamboyant way. Unfortunate, but in the circumstances, unavoidable." Her smile was mirthless. "It must have been a very unpleasant shock for him, all things considered." She shook her head reflectively. "Don't get me wrong. I'm not waging a big war of the sexes with Gareth. You know me. I'm no ardent women's libber. I enjoy all the little courtesies due my frail sex and I don't believe in polluting the atmosphere by bra-burning. But I am a competent human being and I am a good pilot. I expect to get paid for doing a job according to my ability, not my sex, and if I'm the best one to do a particular job, then I expect to be the one to do it, and that's something Gareth Hammond is going to have to learn and to accept. I won't be less than I am for anyone. I don't expect it of him, and he'd damn well better not expect it of me," she finished on a note of level vehemence.

She looked at her parents. "Gareth came here to enlist your influence with me, didn't he? He thought love might accomplish what his orders couldn't. Are you to restrain my more dangerous impulses by using a little moral blackmail?" Without waiting for an answer, she muttered an imprecation under her breath and walked over to the sink to dump the remains of her coffee.

"I'm going to change these clothes before they grow to my skin," she announced. "Then I'm going for a drive, unless you need the car for anything this afternoon, Mom. I'll catch lunch and dinner somewhere. Expect me when you see me."

The door swung gently shut behind her. Daniel let out an audible low whistle. "Miri, my love, I foresee fireworks ahead. We should never have named her Morgain, in spite of your infatuation with the Arthurian tales and championship of Morgan le Fay. We've spawned a witch. She could almost have been in the room with us last night." He gave his deeply thoughtful wife a crooked grin. "D'you think she has the place bugged?"

"Nooo," Miri drawled, a strange grin stealing over her face. "No, but she sure does seem to be able to read his mind sometimes, doesn't she?" She gave a little chuckle but would be drawn no further.

CHAPTER V

Morgain stripped and showered with efficient speed. She dried, dusted herself with powder, and slipped into fresh underclothes with practiced hands. Her hair was pulled into its cascading ponytail atop her head, and she didn't bother with makeup except for a touch of lipgloss and a faint stroke of eye shadow.

It was Sunday, so she bypassed her favorite vacation attire of shorts and scruffy tennis shoes, choosing instead a cool blue sleeveless dress and white thong sandals. The dress covered her bruised shoulders, which were still sore, but they were already healing, the bruising beginning to yellow at the edges. In spite of medical scoffing she regularly took extra vitamin C, and whether it had to do with the self-dosing or not, she never caught cold and her small cuts and bruises always healed with startling rapidity.

With a lightweight acrylic sport shawl that her mother had crocheted for her over her arm and carrying a small white leather purse, she went to find her parents. They were still in the kitchen. They broke off their low-toned conversation when the door swung open. She arched an amused eyebrow at them.

"I'm going now. When John calls, tell him I'll be at the field tomorrow at the regular show time. If anyone else calls, I'm gone and you don't know where or when I'll be back, which is only the simple truth, isn't it?" She blew them a light kiss, and moments later they heard the car's engine roar to life.

When Morgain left the driveway of her parents' home she really had no destination in mind. She only knew that she craved solitude. She wanted to get away from everyone who knew her and all associations with Gareth Hammond. She was battered and bruised in more than a physical sense. Gareth had kept her off-balance ever since they first met, and it was a new and uncomfortable experience for her. She desperately needed breathing space.

She almost decided to seek physical seclusion, to go to a place long favorite with her, overlooking the river, where she had gone before when blue-deviled; but upon reflection she regretfully discarded this option. The way to the river involved a rather arduous climb and an undignified scramble at the end, suitable neither to her mode of dress nor the condition of her shoulder muscles and wrists.

That left a second option, to lose herself in the anonymity of a crowd. There was a strong appeal in this latter course, because when she really came to consider the matter, she was not at all sure she was ready to think about the events of the past few days in any depth. Right now her most fervent wish was to scurry back to San Francisco and put Gareth Hammond out of sight and out of mind, if not permanently (for she knew in her bones that he was not going to allow that until they had had their final reckoning), at least for a time of grace. He stalked her with the relentless passion of the true hunter, and she needed time to rally her defenses.

So, she nodded to herself decisively. She would drive to the city, and there, even though it was Sunday, she would find divertisement and wipe away the memory of a lean body, warm persuasive lips, and angry words—for a time!

The highway was good and practically deserted, allowing her to make excellent time. The natural reflexes that made her such a good pilot came to the fore automatically, to imbue her driving with the same passionless concentration and smooth expertise that characterized her flying. By the time she had reached the city the combined effects of practiced mental discipline and the welcome knowledge of the sheer physical distance she had put between herself and Gareth had restored much of her normal equanimity.

A belated lunch consisted of two mustard-and-sauerkraut-smothered hot dogs consumed in a small, wooded park, one of many that dotted the city, the whole washed down by ice-chilled cola. Morgain sat on the slatted wooden bench, beneath the shade of the dusty-leaved sycamore, munching the ice from the sagging paper cup that had held her drink, and thoughtfully contemplated her sandaled feet and bare toes. In spite of her unvoiced resolution *not* to think about Gareth, he crept, unbidden and insidiously, into her thoughts. The long, free stride of a man walking his dog past her bench, the sheen of the sun on night-black hair . . . drat the man! Must she see him everywhere and in every chance-met male who crossed her path?

She crumpled the empty cup with an irritated gesture and tossed it with graceful accuracy into a nearby waste receptacle. There was usually an afternoon Pops concert put on by the local symphony, and that, perhaps followed by a dinner at one of her favorite restaurants, would divert her traitorous mind from its wearying treadmill of Gareth-awareness.

The concert was enjoyable and providentially provided

the added benefit of companionship for dinner. During the intermission she was hailed by a group, mostly male, of friends she'd known since her nursery-school days. They swept her into their orbit, and she joined the laughing, chattering group for an enjoyable orgy of reminiscence and catching up. They were celebrating the engagement of two of the members of the group, and it was a lighthearted gathering that dined and danced.

While she was dancing with Dave Benson, Morgain caught sight of the watch on his wrist and clucked at the time. When he escorted her back to the table, she began to make her farewells, explaining that she was working tomorrow and needed a reasonably early night. Amid groans and reproaches she saw Dave and Mike Devane conferring and was half prepared when Dave announced that he'd escort her home, Mike would follow in his car to pick him up at her house. Dave masterfully overrode Morgain's protests that it wasn't necessary with the unanswerable, "I know it's not, but I want to do it." Morgain laughingly and gracefully gave in.

The ride home saw a continuation of the easy, comfortable camaraderie she and Dave had always enjoyed. They were old friends and had dated on a casual basis through most of high school. When Dave parked in her parents' driveway and handed her out of the car, it was natural to slip a companionable arm around his waist while his friendly arm came down at the back of her shoulders to guide her up to the front door. The lights from Mike's car as it pulled into the driveway threw their linked figures into prominence, giving them an illusory intimacy that thinned the lips of the man sitting silently on the porch with Morgain's parents.

"How about going out to dinner with me tomorrow

116

night, Morgain?" Dave was urging. "We've still got a lot of catching up to do, and there wasn't much time to talk privately with that lot around tonight. I didn't know you were back in town or I'd have been around sooner."

Morgain was about to answer in the affirmative when a sudden motion and looming shadow distracted her. She jerked to a halt on the first step of the porch, and froze as a silken drawl carried softly through the night.

"It's a shame, but Morgain has a prior engagement tomorrow night . . . and every other night for the rest of her time here at home."

Morgain's breath hissed sharply through her teeth at this piece of blatant provocation, and she could feel the watchful, *poised* aura emanating from that powerful shadow. Her mouth opened to give the lie to his words, only to close again with a snap as Gareth came out of the shadow of the porch and grasped her hand, drawing her from Dave's lax clasp up the remaining steps, and twisting her close to his body in one smooth maneuver. He pulled her back against his chest and crossed his arms possessively around her, and in his touch Morgain felt the leashed violence simmering in his body. She had the almost telepathic impression that, should she dare to contradict him, his arms would contract with iron-muscled thews to stop the breath in her lungs before the words could be formed and released.

"Morgain?" was Dave's soft question.

She opened her lips to answer him and felt the infinitesimal tightening of Gareth's hold. She swallowed once and spoke in a husky, deceptively quiet voice, "I *am* busy tomorrow night, Dave. I'm sorry." Further, she would not go!

Gareth took over again smoothly. "Thank you for seeing that Morgain got home safely, Dave. I appreciate it. I'm Gareth Hammond, by the way, since Morgain has neglected to introduce us."

He held out one hand to the man who stood awkwardly on the lower step. Morgain tried to take advantage of the momentary breach in Gareth's encircling clasp with an unobtrusive duck and sidle to the right, only to find that Gareth was perfectly capable of containing her with only one arm. Short of engaging in an undignified and revealing pitched battle, she must needs stand, quietly seething, in his grasp.

"I'm Dave Benson," was Dave's stiff rejoinder as he accepted Gareth's handshake.

Morgain noted with wry amusement that there was no conventional "I'm glad to meet you" from either man. Dave stood for a moment more before he gave a barely discernible shrug and stepped down from the step.

"Mike's waiting for me, so I won't keep you any longer. Morgain, I'll call you in a couple of days and maybe we can find a time when you're not working to meet for lunch." A nod and a "Hammond" for Gareth and he turned away.

"Good night, Dave. Tell Mike thanks for me" was all Morgain could force between her clenched teeth. Gareth's good-bye was coolly curt.

Morgain stood in stiff silence until Mike had backed his car out of the driveway and driven off. Then she drew a deep preparatory breath and wriggled slightly to test the firmness of Gareth's continuing hold. When it showed no signs of relaxing, she shifted slightly to throw her weight forward on the balls of her feet, and as Gareth leaned forward in response to the change in balance she drove the point of her right elbow back solidly into his ribs. His arms loosened instinctively as a muffled grunt was forced from him. "A textbook exercise," Morgain chortled silently as she twisted inward and down to the right in a flowing motion, sliding neatly out of Gareth's encircling arms. "To make it just like the exercise Miske demonstrated, I really should clip him behind the right knee and push him down the steps," was her further thought, "but I suppose that would be going too far." She continued her motion. It should have brought her out of reach behind him, but to her stunned surprise a steely fingered hand clamped around her wrist and halted her escape abruptly.

"Going inside so soon, my love?" came the dismayingly unruffled tones. "Aren't you going to say good evening to your mother and father? We've been sitting out here on the porch enjoying the night air and a long cool drink."

Morgain went rigid.

"Good evening, Mother. Good evening, Father." Her voice was carefully composed and neutral. "I hope the mosquitoes and gnats haven't bothered either of you," she said, leaving the pious hope that they had bled Gareth white floating unspoken but nonetheless fervent in the air. He chuckled richly, but his grip around her wrist didn't loosen a fraction.

"Do sit for a while with us, Morgain, my love, and tell us about your afternoon and evening." While he spoke he propelled her into the dimly seen wicker couch placed across from the chairs currently occupied by her amused parents. When she was seated, Gareth released his stranglehold on her wrist and sat skin-close to her, draping a pinioning arm across the back of her shoulders.

Even in her rage she noted that he was careful not to bear heavily on her abused shoulders, positioning his arm so that it lay behind the bruised area and cupping her upper arm rather than the point of her shoulder with a caressing hand. His fingers stroked gently but absently up and down the skin of her inner arm as she relaxed slightly until she realized that with each stroke he was also brushing lightly against the side of her breast.

"Gareth!" she hissed in strangled fury.

"Hmmm? Did you say something, my love?" He bent his head solicitously near, managing to pull her even closer against his hard body. "I believe you were going to tell us what you did today."

By now Morgain was blind to the dangers of further provoking Gareth. In sickeningly dulcet tones she began to embroider her day. She described with glowing enthusiasm the concert and enlarged on her delight at joining in celebration with her friends.

"Barbara and Brian have finally decided to get married, Mom. Derek and Steve, Jean and Bob Murphy, and of course Dave and Mike were helping them celebrate. We've all known each other for a donkey's age, Gareth, childhood chums and all that." Her voice was deliberately nostalgic as she continued. "It's at times like these when you realize how much old times mean to you. All the shared memories and fund of happy experiences . . ." She lifted her hand and gestured expressively, managing at the same time to move his hand away from its disturbing contact with her breast.

"Barbara and Brian grew up together, just like Dave and I did, you know." Morgain's tone was confiding. "They dated off and on in high school and then went away to college at opposite ends of the country. But they both came back here to work . . . she's a nurse and he's a bank management trainee . . . and they just picked up where they'd left off."

She spoke as if merely thinking her thoughts aloud. "I'll have to bid my trips so that I can come home for their wedding. Barbara wants me to be a bridesmaid and Dave is to be a groomsman." She allowed a slow smile to curve her mouth. She didn't know whether Gareth could see her expression very well in the dimness, but it wouldn't hurt to add all the extra touches possible. She also allowed a tiny sigh to escape her, a mere exhalation of breath, and knew that it, at least, had registered by his slight tensing.

Evidently her mother felt it was time to take a hand in the proceedings, because she clinked the ice in her glass slightly and said gently, "I'm going to get myself a refill. Come with me, Morgain, dear, and we'll bring fresh drinks for everyone. Some of the lemon meringue pie I made this afternoon might taste good too. Would you like some, Gareth? I know I don't have to ask Daniel . . . he never turns down pie in any flavor."

She began to rise but was neatly forestalled by Gareth. He rose to his feet, impelling Morgain up with him at the same time in as neat a feat of levitation as she'd ever seen, gesturing with his free hand for Miri Kendrick to remain seated.

"No, don't get up. Morgain and I will do the honors. I'm sure her domestic skills will stretch to cutting and serving the pie, and I can cope with the drinks. Daniel, the same again for you, too?"

Barely waiting for Daniel's assent, Gareth urged Morgain toward the front door. The hand he placed on the back of her neck might have looked loverlike, but Morgain had the uncomfortable sensation that she was going to be picked up by the scruff of the neck and shaken like a rag toy at any moment. For a panicky moment her courage deserted her, and she fought the urge to bolt for the bathroom—it having the only door in the house with an operable lock—and slam it safely shut behind her.

She discarded that impulse regretfully. If he didn't catch her before she got there . . . his reflexes seemed to be as good as her own . . . he was perfectly capable of taking the door off the hinges while her mother and father stood by in mild amazement.

They reached the kitchen, and Morgain diverted toward the refrigerator. He caught her with contemptuous ease and pulled her into a bone-cracking embrace that plastered her firmly up against the whole hard length of him. His kiss was all-consuming, and while it lasted she forgot she hated him or loved him or *whatever* it was that she felt for him . . . she simply *felt*! It was an astounding experience, indescribable and unduplicable. All the anger and passion they roused in each other went into that kiss, and when it was over they stood panting for breath with a full yard of space between them.

Gareth was the first to speak, his voice rasping and deep. "This is a *private* war. Keep the boys out of the line of fire or they may get hurt!"

"Are you by any chance referring to Dave?" Morgain questioned him loftily.

"Dave, Mike, Steve, Derek, Tige, or any other irrelevant name you choose to drag past me as a red herring. Be warned, Morgain. If one of your tame tomcats gets in my way, he'll get hurt, so if you have friendly feelings for any one of them, do him a favor and keep away from him."

Perhaps it was a trick of the light in the kitchen, but for a moment he could swear her hair glowed red. Her voice was clear and soft, each word enunciated with cutting precision.

"I was not aware that I had given you the right to express an opinion about, much less dictate, with whom I will or will not associate. As we say in pilot talk, Gareth, hear me loud and clear." She was quivering perceptibly with the intensity of her outrage, intensely beautiful, infinitely desirable, and madder than a cat with its tail caught in a door. "I will go out with *whomever* I choose, *whenever* I choose, and you can just, just . . . lump it!" she finished, sputtering inelegantly but graphically. Her hands were tightly clenched, and he had the distinct impression that if there had been a rock handy, he would now be sporting a lump of no mean proportions. An injudicious grin was his final mistake of the evening. With a look that spoke volumes concerning his ancestry, and his probably destination in the afterlife, Morgain swung gracefully about and exited the kitchen. No queen could have swept out with greater hauteur and stiff-backed disdain. The door closed ever so softly behind her. Gareth stood gazing thoughtfully at the blank panels of the door, waiting. Ten seconds later came the vicious slam of a door somewhere in the house. It rattled every window and made the china chatter. He gave a rueful chuckle and removed the pie from the refrigerator.

He could feel the silent inquiry from Morgain's parents as he carried the tray out to the porch. Miri relieved him of his burden and distributed its contents, leaning the empty tray against the porch railing before she sat down again. They ate and drank in silence.

"That was delicious, Miri. No wonder Daniel never turns down any of your pie." Gareth's voice was that of the courteous guest, no more. Then the wry laughter could be contained no longer. "Daniel, I believe I have committed a tactical error of some magnitude. Morgain is more than a little peeved with me."

"If you plan to have anything to do with the Ryan women on a steady basis, you'll find that's not an uncommon occurrence," was Daniel's dry rejoinder. "The first year Miri and I were married I collected more broken crockery off the floor than was ever set on the table for meals."

"Daniel!" Miri said warningly.

"Of course, now there are plastic, unbreakable dishes, so you can avoid that hazard from the start," Daniel continued in a meditative tone. "Morgain has a pretty fair arm though . . . all that softball in high school, you know . . . and if she threw a plate at you like a discus, it might be fairly lethal if it connected. Perhaps paper plates would be best. You'd have to drink your soup pretty quickly . . ."

It was hard to tell whether the muffled sounds coming from the shadowy form that was Miri Kendrick were indignation or amusement.

"Well now, Daniel, since you've had a long and obviously successful association with Ryan women, could I prevail upon you to offer a novice some hints and advice on how to go on?" Gareth requested humbly.

Daniel laughed. "Well now, my boy, I wouldn't want to deprive you of any of the perils and pleasures inherent in Ryan taming."

"Daniel!"

This time there was no mistaking Miri's emotional tenor. Indignation made each word crackle as she rose. "When you *gentlemen* are through indulging in your sophomoric humor at the expense of my daughter and myself, you may return the dishes to the kitchen. I

. . ." Her tone was the unconscious but exact duplicate of her daughter's icy enunciation earlier in the kitchen. "I am retiring for the night. Good evening." She swept gracefully into the house.

There was a long, expressive silence as the door closed gently behind her until, in delayed but faithful echo, came the resounding vibration of another crockery-rattling slam.

Daniel sighed. "Just goes to prove that there's no fool like an old fool, Gareth. You'd think after thirty years of happy marriage I would have learned that sticking one's foot in one's mouth is both profitless and damned uncomfortable."

Gareth chuckled. "If we're indulging in platitudes, I could say that misery loves company, and there's plenty of room in my doghouse. Your daughter and your wife seem to have a most unfortunate reaction to the notion of being tamed." He unconsciously rubbed the top of his right foot as it rested aslant his left knee.

"I can show you a scar on my shin that ought to have reminded me of that," Daniel muttered.

"Were you dancing at the time?" asked Gareth sympathetically.

"You too?"

The two men burst into resounding laughter, and to the two women in their separate rooms, the masculine hilarity drifting through the opened windows was additional gratuitous fuel piled on already brightly blazing tempers. A glint in each blue eye boded ill for their respective males in days to come.

Morgain had been alternately pacing and pausing to glare at the door through which she had swept in such fury after the scene, if such a mild word could do justice to the

125

strength of the feelings she had unleashed in the kitchen. Had there truly been any powers of witchcraft extant in the female line of her family, her fervent imprecations would have brought down on Gareth's unfortunate head such an amazing variety of physical ailments and distressing symptoms as to make him a fit subject for a medical journal.

While Gareth was consuming his pie Morgain was debating the relative merits of drawing and quartering (although she wasn't certain exactly what it entailed, it sounded *suitable)* versus incarceration in the Iron Maiden. When he was graceless enough to laugh with such unrepentant enjoyment instead of slinking away in decent discomfiture, she decided that those fates were too merciful and quick for the likes of him! She would ask Eric Sorgenson to take her to dinner at the hotel tomorrow night. Eric was six feet, six inches in his bare feet and muscled like a plow horse. He was an expert in self-defense and an ex-major in the Marine Corps, a combat veteran with well-earned decorations for valor. He was also a very good friend, and he owed her a favor. To make his qualifications absolutely perfect, he was engaged to one of her close friends, and Cathy had as wicked a sense of humor as Morgain herself. Cathy would lend Eric with the greatest goodwill after Morgain had explained the circumstances.

"A private war, is it?" Morgain murmured, and smiled a chilling smile.

Morgain was jerked from her pleasurable musings by a soft tap on the door. "Who is it?" she hissed.

"Mom."

Morgain flung wide the door. Her mother slid, almost furtively, into the room, and Morgain gaped at her in surprise. Miri perched herself on Morgain's bed, curling her legs beneath her.

"I have come for a council of war," she announced grimly, patting the bed beside her invitingly. Morgain sank down weakly beside her mother and awaited revelation.

"Your father has so far forgotten family loyalty as to agree with Gareth that Ryan females need 'taming,'" Miri stated evenly, her eyes flashing dangerously.

Morgain rolled her eyes heavenward and growled softly.

"Exactly," agreed Miri. She looked at her daughter appraisingly, lapsed into obvious thought for a long second, and began to speak again. "Morgain, I am your mother. You can speak frankly and freely to me. Do you want Gareth Hammond?" She held up a restraining hand, stilling the heated denial that was about to tumble from Morgain's lips. "Wait. If you have not seriously considered this question in depth and detail, do so now, before you answer. Consider the radical change in your life-style, consider the irritations of living with such a . . . a . . . dominantly masculine male, and"—here her eye took on a distinctly feminine twinkle that would have appalled her husband—"consider the fringe benefits."

Morgain's broad grin matched her mother's. "Mmm, yes. It's the fringe benefits that get you every time." Her face sobered, and her eyes took on an introspective blindness. A long silence ensued. Miri seemed sunk in her own reflections as well. Finally Morgain stirred. Miri regarded her daughter expectantly.

Morgain looked at her mother. "Yes, damn him," she nodded her head in irritated surrender. "Yes, I do want him. But not"—her face hardened with firm resolve—"on his terms."

"Of course not!" snapped her mother. "That wouldn't be good for either of you. Gareth is not the sort of man to enjoy or be captivated by a biddable female. Bland fare soon ceases to titillate the palate. All right, what's your next step? What are you doing about tomorrow night?"

"I'm going to borrow Eric from Cathy for dinner at the hotel," Morgain admitted smugly.

Miri hugged her daughter. "Excellent. You can count on me to put a spike in your father's guns whenever necessary, if he shows signs of becoming an active participant. I think we'll allow him to offer advice anytime he wishes . . . that's liable to be more helpful to us than to Gareth. If I were you, however, I'd have Eric pick you up at Cathy's. Go there to shower and change after you finish your last flight. Tell me what you want to wear and I'll drop it off at Cathy's on my way to the grocery store tomorrow morning. Leave me to handle Gareth when he comes to the house. The timing of the confrontation will be critical. Hmmm, I have it." She snapped her fingers. "Call me from Cathy's to let me know what time you'll be eating dinner and I'll arrange for your father to let Gareth know that you're dining with ANOTHER MAN at the hotel in time for you to be about half finished with the meal. Then he'll have plenty of time to get there to see you go in to dance with Eric."

"Oh, Mom, must I?" Morgain groaned. "Eric dances like a tank. It's beyond me how any man who is as agile and as adept in so many forms of self-defense can be such a total disaster on the dance floor. I can't cuddle up to Eric convincingly while I'm trying to keep my toes intact. Cathy swears that she's going to put in the marriage vows

128

that Eric promise to love, honor, cherish, and never set foot on the dance floor with her again."

Miri giggled. "That bad, huh? I thought your father was the world's worst."

"Daddy doesn't weigh 250 pounds. Well, I suppose Gareth is worth the risk," she continued rather doubtfully. "In any event, I can't let Gareth get away with thinking he can dictate to me with impunity. I made him no commitments, nor he me." Her wrath began to kindle again. "How *dare* he say what he did to Dave?" Morgain's voice was laced with mockery. " 'Thank you for seeing that Morgain got home safely, Dave. *I* appreciate it.' Who gave him the right to appreciate it?" she snarled.

Miri's voice was amused. "I don't think Gareth is the type of man to wait to be given the right. And you know something else," she assessed shrewdly, "I think jealousy is a brand-new emotion for him. I'll bet you my new waffle iron that he's never cared enough about a woman before to try and dominate her so thoroughly." She giggled girlishly. "Perhaps that's why he's making such a botch of it . . . not enough practice."

This observer's viewpoint of their courtship—for suddenly Morgain realized that this was what it amounted to—was illuminating. "Do you really think he was jealous?" she questioned her mother.

"My dear, he came to the house this afternoon right after he and John got in from Buckeye, and the interrogation your father and I endured when he found you were gone stopped just short of a full-scale inquisition. Had you been gone long? Where did you go and whom were you with? Were you going to meet anyone and when would you be home? He seemed to get remarkably little pleasure from any of our answers, and I think he would have sat

129

out on that porch like a heavy father waiting for his only daughter to come home from her first date until morning if necessary. When you and Dave got out of the car and came toward the house, the air fairly sizzled around him. Personally, I think Dave had a lucky escape. I don't believe Gareth would balk at a little physical contact if the mood hit him."

"Too true. Why do you think I chose Eric to borrow? Even Gareth wouldn't go up against him. I don't want anyone hurt . . . I just want to prove my point." Her expression was decidedly rueful. "You know, whenever I fantasized about the man I'd eventually fall in love with, I certainly never dreamed about a bullheaded, chauvinistic, infuriating man like Gareth has turned out to be. Do you think I'm an unconscious masochist or just a glutton for punishment?"

"I think you've got yourself a special man, darling." Miri grinned impishly at her daughter and continued, "But then, I happen to think you're someone special myself, and you're a good match for him. I have every confidence that you'll give as good as you get, and while your life in the near future won't be peaceful, it will certainly be stimulating."

Morgain laughed delightedly. "If anything, I fear you understate the case, Mother, dear." She yawned suddenly. "Oh, my, 'scuse me. It's been a *long* day."

"And so will tomorrow be," finished her mother. "Time for your beauty sleep, dear." She patted her daughter's hand and rose from the bed, smiling down fondly upon her heavy-eyed daughter, who had flopped gracefully backward to stretch full length across the coverlet. "Poor Gareth," Miri mused almost inaudibly. "I don't think he realizes fully even yet just what's hit him."

Morgain slept the sleep of the just that night, dreamless and deep. When she arose in the brightening morning, there was a smile on her lips that would not have looked amiss on the mouth of Torquemada just before he cranked the rack up another notch. She paced to the bedroom window and swung open the screen to thrust her head out and breathe deeply of the crisp air. She twisted her body gingerly from the waist, testing the extent of residual stiffness remaining from her battering on Saturday. A few grimaces notwithstanding, she persisted with limbering exercises until she regained her natural litheness of movement and after the beneficial hot shower felt reasonably ready to fight her weight in outraged mink.

She entered the kitchen with a jaunty swing and smiled cheerily at her parents.

"Good morning, Mom. Good morning, Dad. Isn't it a lovely day? My, I'm hungry enough to eat a giraffe, neck and all. Mmm. Sausages and scrambled eggs with buttermilk biscuits. Marvelous."

She was helping herself liberally while she spoke, and her blithe tone raised her father's eyebrows to his hairline. Morgain at her blandest augured ill for someone, and Gareth was the most likely target. Ah, well, he was a big boy, and Daniel figured he was well able to take care of himself. He silently poured a glass of freshly squeezed orange juice and handed it to Morgain.

"Thanks, Dad." She drank a satisfying swallow. "Ah, nectar of the gods. How people can be content with that frozen stuff when the real thing is available is beyond me. Do you know, I even had one of the pilots tell me that he preferred the frozen concentrate? Said it tasted more like the 'real thing' to him." She chuckled at the absurdity. She was bubbling with the joy of living. It roistered through her veins and overflowed in happy mirth, inviting her parents to share the wonder of being alive and young with her. Colors were bright and sharply toned, the air was fresh with morning scent, and the certain knowledge that today she would see Gareth and enter another round of their courtship sparring exhilarated her.

Daniel intercepted several significant glances between his wife and daughter with growing dismay. Long experience taught him that they were up to something. There was an unmistakable aura of smug satisfaction floating over the breakfast dishes, and while he had every confidence that Gareth and Morgain were evenly matched, he was not at all sure that Gareth versus Morgain plus Miri was a fair contest. What Morgain lacked in devious deviltry her mother could easily supply, and a natural fellow-feeling for a poor, beset male rose strongly within him. He also felt somewhat responsible for unwisely provoking Miri last night, perhaps supplying the impetus for her to enter the lists on the side of her daughter. Miri might well have rested content to observe the carnage from the sidelines if he had not succumbed to the impulse to forgo his own neutrality in the border war between the two young people. Unfortunately Gareth had reminded him of his younger self while in hot pursuit of Miri too strongly to enable him to forgo a bit of commiseration and encouragement. He sighed soundlessly. He'd just have to keep his eyes and ears open in the hope that he could catch a hint of what those two had planned. Gareth deserved that much at least.

Morgain chased the last scrap of sausage around her plate, swallowed the final fragrant drop of coffee from her cup, and beamed at her parents.

"Time to go to work. After a meal like this I could do barrel rolls all across the sky. I won't be in for dinner tonight, Mom" she added significantly.

Her mother shot her 'an admonitory look as Morgain grinned widely in contemplation of the evening ahead. Daniel wasn't dense, and it wouldn't do to alert him. A light touch was definitely desirable, and Morgain was too ebullient not to arouse the suspicions of her astute husband. If Daniel knew Miri, Miri also knew Daniel, knew full well that he would warn Gareth if he caught an inkling of their plan. Last night had shown all too clearly where his sympathies lay, and they weren't with his daughter.

Miri remembered her own courtship vividly and, realized that as in her and Daniel's case, an outright win for either side would be disastrous. Only an honorable stalemate would serve. Morgain had too much sense to want to dominate her husband, but neither would she be happy being dominated. In fact, Miri thought, a docile Morgain would be the eighth wonder of the world. As soon as Gareth could be brought to accept the fact, the war would be over. The slogan of the hippies in the 1960s flitted ribaldly through her mind: MAKE LOVE, NOT WAR. She snickered, and both her husband and her daughter looked questioningly at her. Daniel immediately recognized the glint in his wife's eyes, but was at a loss to discover what had sparked off the train of thought.

"Well, I'm off to a hard day slaving over a hot instrument panel," Morgain announced gaily. "Keep the home fires burning, Mom." She left the kitchen humming snatches from *Die Valkyrie* in a shockingly upbeat rhythm.

Morgain made her call to Cathy from a pay phone on

her way to the airport. Cathy was slightly disoriented at first, but the shock of trying to concentrate at such an early hour faded rapidly. She entered into the plan with great zest, as Morgain knew she would.

"Hmm, convincing Eric to cooperate will be the biggest hurdle, Morgain dear. He has all the natural male aversion to doing down one of his own sex, but never fear," Cathy promised, "I'll deliver him primed and ready this evening at my house." She growled in a gutteral German accent, "Ve haf ways of assuring your cooperation. . . ."

"Hooray for the weaker sex," chortled Morgain. "Thanks, Cath. I'll see you this evening about five thirty."

Morgain was well pleased with the day's course. John handled her as he would handle a vial of fulminate of mercury and flinched every time she smiled at him. He even broke into a light sweat when she casually asked him if Terry Black still had his crop duster. Ken cornered her as she headed out to the plane for her second run of the day.

"Say, Morgain, what in the world is wrong with John? He's as jumpy as though he expected a tap on the shoulder from the IRS saying 'Uncle Sam wants to have a word with you.' Have you been giving him a hard time?"

Her answering gaze was limpid with innocence. "But Ken, why ever would I want to give John a hard time? I haven't laid a glove on him, as the saying goes. Your imagination seems to be working overtime, dear brother, and if John has a guilty conscience, I'm *sure* it's no concern of mine." She smiled most sweetly at him and walked on to her waiting plane.

Ken, with a finely honed instinct for self-preservation engendered by two years of marriage and many years of being Morgain's brother, decided that it was not intelligent to stick one's hand deliberately into a wasp's nest. Sensibly, he went about his own business. Ever since Morgain had started dating Gareth there had been storms and he figured that this, too, shall pass, but until it did, there were always things he could find to do elsewhere.

One of the fringe benefits of having a wife was that he had a direct pipeline to all the latest gossip without the hazard of having to inquire about it himself. A simple "What's going on between Morgain and Gareth?" to Jenny over the supper table should elicit all the latest information with no further effort on his part. Even having a baby had had no measurable effect on his Jenny's ability to garner the latest intelligence about who was doing what to whom, and why! Well pleased with himself and his ruminations, Ken broke into a cheery whistle . . . "She'll Be Coming 'Round the Mountain," to be exact.

All was going smoothly. Mòrgain hied herself to Cathy's at the appointed time, to find her dress and clean underclothes waiting, as prearranged with her mother. After she had showered, she borrowed a light wrap from Cathy and began to arrange her hair and makeup while Cathy perched cross-legged on the bed and plied her with rapid-fire questions.

"There wasn't much time to go into detail this morning, Morgain, and I don't know how much I could have retained anyway . . . you know I'm at less than my best at that hour . . . but I think I got the gist of it. Correct me if I'm wrong, but you want Eric to kind of loom over you protectively but not to actually 'fold, spindle or mutilate' Gareth?" (Cathy worked for a computer company.)

"How poetic," gurgled Morgain. "No, I don't want Gareth even slightly bent. It's just that Gareth and I are engaged in . . . mmm . . . sort of a private war and I felt it was time to call up reinforcement troops. Eric sprang to mind as a battalion in his own right."

"Well, if it's war, I guarantee that you'll have earned a Purple Heart by the end of the evening if you plan to lead Eric out on the dance floor."

"I know," sighed Morgain as she smoothed eye shadow over her upper lids. "I danced with him at your engagement party, remember? Believe me, if it weren't for the fact that six-foot-six brick outhouses are thin on the ground around here, *nothing* could induce me to set foot on the dance floor with Eric again. That tells you right now how I feel about Gareth. I have come to the reluctant conclusion that I love him." But with those words her chin came up and her nostrils flared with temper. "But I'll be damned if I let him ride roughshod over me. He's arrogant and entirely too sure of himself. He thinks that he can just snap his fingers and I'll leap meekly to do his bidding—"

Her burgeoning tirade was interrupted by Cathy's outright laugh. "He must also be mentally deficient if he sees you as meek."

Morgain grinned. "Well, no, definitely not mentally deficient," she admitted. "He just wants to be boss. He has had a bad case of the 'I am master of my fate and yours too' syndrome, and while I don't mind a touch of it now and then, a steady diet goes against the grain. When I marry I want a working partnership, not a master-minion setup. It's just taking me awhile to bring Gareth around to that opinion too." She continued thoughtfully. "I don't think Gareth has ever thought of a woman in those terms before . . . as a partner rather than a plaything, I mean. I would be surprised to find that he has any women friends, using friend in the fullest sense of the word

. . . someone you like, trust, and can depend upon."

She slipped into her dress, stood motionless as Cathy zipped the zipper up the long, smooth length of her back, and then began to make a neat bundle of her discarded clothes and tennis shoes.

"I'll leave these in my car. Eric can bring me back here this evening after our scenario has run its course. Er . . . how much of the situation did you explain to Eric?"

Cathy chuckled. "Well, at first I almost decided not to explain much at all. As I said, Eric has all the natural instincts of loyalty to his sex, even one he's never met before, and though he's about to join the ranks of the committed himself, the old bachelor instincts die hard. But then, I realized that if I just left him with the impression that you wanted him to be a shield against a man who was . . . ahem . . . making things a little hot for you, Eric might be a little overzealous in his protection and your Gareth might indeed get a little bent or folded. Eric likes you very much, Morgain, and for some reason he thinks of women as the weaker sex, needing protection from the big, cruel world," Cathy's brown eyes sparkled mischievously, and Morgain joined her in purely feminine chuckles. Like many big men Eric was very solicitous of weaker beings, always displaying an innate chivalry that his fiancée privately found touching and appealing.

"So, much as it went against the grain to expose the workings of our feminine stratagems, I told him as much as I knew, that you ah . . . liked Gareth very much, but he was being a bit too possessive, too soon, and you merely wanted to slow the pace a bit."

"How did Eric take that revelation?" was Morgain's interested query.

"Suspiciously unsurprised, I thought," Cathy replied,

137

"I wonder if he's heard something. You know, Dave hasn't been backward in expressing his opinion of Gareth Hammond, and I've always thought he'd be more than willing to heat up the relationship between the two of you if you ever gave him the slightest encouragement."

"I know, but he's just never appealed to me that way." Morgain smiled a trifle ruefully. "As the saying goes, we're just good friends. That and the fact that he's nowhere up to Gareth's weight precludes my asking him to help me out. Gareth's already shipped Tige Anderson off to San Francisco for an unspecified period of exile because I tried to put him on the front line of our private war, as Gareth so quaintly put it."

Cathy whistled softly at this further revelation. "He really clears the decks for action, doesn't he?"

"I wonder if he even gave Tige time to pack?" was Morgain's oblique agreement with this perceptive observation. She would have said more, but Cathy's mother stuck her head in the door and announced Eric's arrival, her eyes twinkling. She was an older version of her daughter and viewed the world with a contagious amusement that had endeared her to her daughter's many friends.

"The stalking goat has arrived" was Mrs. MacHenry's blithe announcement as she gazed benignly at her daughter and her daughter's best friend.

"Oh, Aunt Jean, I doubt if Eric would like to hear himself called a *goat*," Morgan said. "Surely more of a knight in shining armor, a paladin, perhaps." Her tone oozed mock horror. "Goats are smelly and ill-tempered. What a way to speak of your future son-in-law. It casts such aspersions on your daughter's taste in men."

The three women broke into whoops of laughter and went to confront the calmly waiting Eric.

138

CHAPTER VI

It was the last time Morgain laughed with real merriment that night, and as she lay in bed much later, flexing her aching toes, she considered how a brilliantly conceived plan could go so disastrously (from her point of view) awry.

They had gone to the hotel for dinner, and Eric had played his part of solicitous escort to the hilt. In his own way Eric had as devilish a sense of humor as his bride-to-be and was no mean actor when he put his mind to it. They were ordering dinner when Gareth entered the dining room and surveyed the occupants. Eric had immediately begun to flirt outrageously with her, and Morgain had looked at him in surprise until the familiar tingle at the back of her neck gave her a clue to the reason for his abrupt change in manner.

"Eric," she hissed warningly, "I don't want to make him madly jealous, you idiot! I just want to exert my independence a bit."

"What's more independent than—" Eric broke off abruptly, and Morgain didn't need the warm hand that laid itself so possessively on her shoulder or the masculine lips that kissed her firmly on the lips to tell her who stood by her chair.

Morgain looked up in shock at Gareth as he watched Eric rise to his full, awesome height across the table. Not a flicker of expression crossed his face until Eric was completely erect. An amused, unholy smile spread across Gareth's mouth. He held out his hand to the other man. Morgain watched Eric's eyes widen and then narrow in speculation. The two men shook hands, and she listened with horror as Gareth spoke.

"Good evening, Sorgenson. I'm very happy to meet you. Sorry I'm late, but the plane was delayed in getting in and I had to wait until it had landed," Gareth said smoothly.

Morgain shot a suspicious look at Eric, thoughts of some sort of masculine conspiracy rioting through her bewildered brain, but his face was as uncomprehending as her own.

"It was good of you to bring Morgain on to the hotel," he continued as he pulled out the chair next to Morgain and sat down. Eric dazedly resumed his seat as Gareth swept on, "But of course you understand. Since I had promised Morgain her ring today, I naturally had to wait until the courier who was bringing it arrived. I don't break my promises, do I, Morgain my darling?" Morgain heard the underlying steel.

"My ring?" was all Morgain could croak.

Gareth glanced around them and smiled, inviting Eric's masculine understanding. "Well, I had planned on a slightly more romantic setting when I slid it onto your finger, but if you can't wait to see it . . ." He suited actions to words. He grasped her left hand, removed a magnificent platinum and diamond ring from his coat pocket, and slid it smoothly on her ring finger. He lifted her hand to his mouth and sensuously kissed the knuckle of that finger.

She felt his tongue-tip flick against her skin. He captured her stunned gaze, holding her eyes as he said significantly, "Sealed *on* with a kiss."

Morgain knew she must be gulping like a stranded fish, but she was beyond speech. A hasty look at Eric showed his eyes were twinkling. She had the depressed feeling that he was just barely restraining himself from bursting into loud guffaws.

Gareth spoke again, urbane and bland, still holding Morgain's left hand, his fingers stroking the back of her hand softly and deliberately. "I thought your fiancée was joining us tonight, Sorgenson, for the celebration. Perhaps she was delayed? I've been looking forward to meeting *all* of Morgan's friends, and I understand Cathy is one of her best and oldest friends, since nursery-school days, hmmm?"

Morgain nodded her head numbly, coherent speech still beyond her. She was not at all surprised when Cathy appeared moments later in the doorway of the dining room. The two men rose politely to their feet, and Cathy sat down across from Morgain, shooting her friend a rueful and apologetic glance as she did so. Morgain mouthed "How?" to Cathy and received only an "I have no idea" shrug of the shoulders in answer.

Eric introduced Cathy to Gareth, who smiled charmingly and said that he was glad she had been able to join them after all. Gareth summoned the waiter to the table and they ordered dinner, with Gareth's addition of celebratory champagne.

Gareth overrode her feeble protests that she had to work the next morning and shouldn't have any alcohol, and the look in his eyes as he made his toast to her sent a rush of heat from the pit of her stomach flashing through her body to dye every inch of her skin a warm, rosy hue. It was the look of a panther before he takes the first bite, predatory and very, very hungry.

In theory it should have made her angry or apprehensive, but something feminine and feline in her nature treacherously purred, deep at the core of her inmost self. Consciously or not, she had accelerated the pace of the "war" between them by defying Gareth's edict. He had warned her that it was a private war, and she had deliberately ignored his stricture. Now he had moved decisively to insure that it would remain their private war.

How he knew about Eric (and Cathy, for that matter) was a minor puzzle. Probably she had her father to thank for that, but the speed and devastating expertise with which he turned her own plot against her was ominous in the extreme. Unless she made a scene in front of everyone in the dining room (and she wasn't at all sure that would accomplish anything anyway, judging from the gleam in Gareth's eyes), she was now an engaged woman. A fait accompli is drattedly hard to fight, and how can one say "No!" to a question that has never been asked?

To add to Morgain's discomfort it seemed that a convocation of all the biggest gossips in the town were eating dinner at the hotel that evening, and drawn by the air of celebration and the all too obvious bucket with its cooled bottle of champagne, they all stopped by the table, noses atwitch. By the time dinner was over Morgain realized that not only would there be no need to place a formal announcement in the newspaper, but her parents would probably already have been informed of their daughter's forthcoming nuptials by the time she got home.

The rest of the evening at the hotel was mainly a blur with occasional highlights, such as the time she warily went out on the dance floor with Eric, to find that he had not measurably improved since the last time he had mashed her feet at Cathy's engagement party, and had, in fact, probably gained a pound or two.

It didn't help to see Gareth lightly and deftly twirl by with Cathy in his arms, her blissful expression indicating her delight in the graceful expertise of her partner. When Gareth danced with Morgain next, he murmured lovingly in her ear, "I feel my foot has been amply revenged," and adroitly thwarted her attempt to kick him in the shin by the simple expedient of pulling her so tightly against his body that she could feel the whole strong length of him burning against her.

"Gareth!" she gasped in shock. The room was shadowed, but not *that* dark, and she could feel eyes being drawn to them like so many magnets lining up iron filings. He relaxed his hold slightly, and she eased away from him, dancing more sedately, though it was a mere matter of degree since he had both his arms around her waist and her arms were still looped about his neck, where he had placed them when they first went out on the dance floor.

He began to nuzzle her ear, and one hand moved caressingly up and down her spine while the other dropped lower to splay out over the back of her hips, just below her waist. She stiffened automatically, but the music and the two glasses of champagne, combined with the insidious physical chemistry working between them, defeated her momentarily. With a purr deep in her throat she tucked her head under his chin and plastered her upper body against him so that her breasts flattened against his chest wall.

Being so close to him, she couldn't miss his involuntary indrawn breath or the sudden slam of his accelerated heartbeat, and a wicked smile curved her mouth. She was really playing with fire, but some reckless demon drove her on. She'd lost a major battle in the dining room, but she hadn't conceded the war!

She was not surprised when Gareth announced that it was time for them to leave when the dance changed to a faster tempo, using her early show time in the morning as excuse enough. When Morgain muttered something incoherent about her car, he blandly informed her that he'd already arranged to have it returned to her house and, in fact, it should be in the driveway already. She didn't miss Eric's admiring look. Chalk one up for male supremacy.

The drive to her house was silent. Gareth evidently saw no need to talk, and for the life of her Morgain couldn't think of any opening that wouldn't immediately put her on the defensive. She started conversations mentally only to find them skittering away as the memory of the feel of Gareth's hard length against her softer body kept obtruding.

When they pulled into the dark driveway of her parents' home, there indeed was the car. Gareth didn't even glance at it. He turned off the ignition, unsnapped his seat belt, reached over and unsnapped Morgain's. He moved along the seat until he was clear of the steering wheel, and with a dextrous twist turned Morgain into his arms so that she lay back, supported by his left arm.

She lay relaxed against him, staring up into his eyes like a hypnotized rabbit. There was moonlight, and the diffuse radiance was enough to show him the moist sheen of her lips and the warm silk texture of her cheek. He lifted a not quite steady hand to gently stroke her throat and, as she arched her neck into his hand, his mouth came down to cover hers.

144

All coherent thought fled from Morgain's mind. *This* was what she was made for, this rapture of his deep, probing kiss. He captured the moan that fluttered in her throat, her whisper of surrender and hunger, accepting it into his mouth as he would a bite of honey, savoring the sweetness fully. When he ran his tongue gently across her lower lip, she shivered, and when his mouth laid kisses across her cheeks and eyelids, her left hand came up to bury itself in the thick dark hair at the back of his head, pulling him back to meet her softly ravenous mouth.

Gareth tilted Morgain into his chest as he kissed her deeply once again, but even if she had noticed the slide of the zipper, she was too engrossed in the sensations that flared through her body to object. Deftly he eased the dress from her shoulders and down past her waist, leaving only the frail lace of her wispy bra as barrier between him and his immediate objective. He released the catch between her breasts, and with gentle hands slid the straps off her shoulders.

He lifted his mouth from hers and laid her back across the hard strength of his left arm, letting his eyes feast on the uncovered richness before him. Her skin was silvered in the moonglow and there were no color tones, only light and dark.

"Oh, God, Morgain, you're so beautiful," he whispered as his mouth moved to taste what his eyes devoured.

Morgain felt an exquisite shock run through her body as his mouth fastened on her breast, his big warm palm shaping and molding it even as his lips sipped and tasted. Her back arched in a reflex motion she couldn't control, and a soft whimper of pleasure forced its way past her parted lips. He kissed his way from one warm crest, pausing in the valley between her breasts to taste with tongue

145

tip, up to lay the same ravishing sensation upon the other waiting peak.

She lost all sense of time. His caressing hands and seeking mouth were her only reality, and the sky could have burned away to dawn for all the notice she took of the outer world. It took her drugged senses some time to assimilate the fact that he had ceased to send her ever deeper into the whirlpool of sensual stimulation, and was instead bringing her gently but relentlessly back to the surface of rational thought.

She could feel his body shudder with the effort he was making to master his own nearly out of control desires, and his words continued to caress her mind, though his hands had ceased to smooth and mold her skin with such passionate possession. She resisted this enforced return to reality. Her hands went up to loop around his neck, seeking to pull his head down again, but the strong muscles of his neck resisted all her efforts to bend him to her once more.

"Love me, Gareth. Please love me," she whispered to him in explicit invitation. Her body burned with a deep, craving ache, and she was nearly mad with wanting him. Instinct was her guide where experience lacked, and his arms tightened convulsively around her for a moment before he forced a hoarse, nearly inarticulate "No!" from the mouth that was buried in her shoulder.

"No!" he repeated almost savagely as he held her away from him and drew in a deep breath. She looked at him in blind bewilderment, unable to understand his rejection. He slipped her bra back on and firmly clipped the front clasp, his knuckles impersonal against the soft swell he had so lately caressed. With shaking fingers Morgain pulled on her dress and submitted to his fingers as they drew the zipper up in one swift motion. Reality was intruding sharply now, and she began to burn with humiliation. The last of her madness drained swiftly away, and the transition to sanity was brutal.

Gareth was still struggling for control, so his voice was harsher than he intended it to be. "The first time I take you, Morgain, it won't be in the front seat of a car."

He meant his words in explanation, but Morgain heard only rejection. For the first time in her life she had offered herself to a man. He was the man she loved, but not a man she understood or even fully trusted. The relationship was too fragile, too new, lacking the depth of tender commitment that would have enabled her to evaluate correctly the meanings underlying the bald words.

Had she understood, she could have measured the depth of Gareth's feelings for her. He was paying in physical anguish for his desire to insure that their first time was good, was satisfying for her. He intended that her initiation at his hands would be more than acrobatic contortions in a cramped car parked in the driveway of her parents' home, but words can be clumsy if the heart does not hear all the shades of meaning.

Gareth spoke love but Morgain heard arrogance. She moved back to her side of the car, her hand fumbling for the handle of the door. As her fingers closed around it, shielded from Gareth's sight by the darkness and her half-turned body, she began to ease it silently upward until she felt the latch release. Even in the dark Gareth was sensitive to her moods, and he made a convulsive grab for her. Only desperation and superb reflexes enabled her to elude him, and her words carried clearly to him as she sprinted toward the door.

"There won't be a *first* time, Gareth!"

He reached the front door a split second after the dead-bolt clicked home, and his frustrated demand that she come back out and listen to him elicited only silence. In a raging temper he drove himself back to the hotel suite, heading for a cold shower and a stiff drink.

Ingrained discipline made Morgain skip the stiff drink, though she could well have done with it, but her shower was prolonged and hot. Reaction had her alternately shivering and fever-flushed as though with ague. Tears of rage and hurt dripped down her cheeks to mingle with the shower droplets. Finally she quit the shower and, wrapped in a bath sheet, went back into her bedroom where the ring Gareth had so firmly thrust on her finger mere hours ago winked balefully at her from the table where she had thrown it.

She held it between thumb and forefinger, watching the prismed fire leap and flicker across the surface of the diamond. It was a lovely ring. With a rueful sigh she laid it on the bedside table. The bath sheet dropped in a damp and crumpled heap at the foot of the bed, and she climbed between the sun-scented cool sheets.

As she expected, sleep was elusive. She plumped her pillows determinedly and shut her eyes, but to no avail. Her wayward mind scurried busily down paths her conscious mind had no wish to tread. She realized that her thumb was unconsciously rubbing her ringless finger, and had her language been audible, it would probably have set the bed linen on fire. She called herself a fool and other uncomplimentary pejoratives, but still her hand reached out with almost a life of its own and lifted the ring from where it lay on the table.

Just for tonight, she promised herself. It slid on her finger as if going home, which of course called immediately to mind the look in Gareth's eyes as he had placed it on her finger, and *that* did nothing for her peace of mind. Was she a fool? She had known the type of man he was from the moment she first laid eyes on him. She had walked right into this situation with her eyes wide open. The Spanish had a word for it: macho. Dominant? That was no bad thing. She had no use for a biddable man, but domineering? That was another kettle of fish indeed.

Morgain was being pulled apart on the rack of her desires. She craved Gareth with a body instinct that she could not seem to control. From the moment she had faced him in the dimness of the hangar she had been aware of him as a man, dangerous but oh, so vital and exciting. She had met men before who attracted her mildly, some who had even caused her to wonder "What would it be like?" but with Gareth she seemed determined to find out!

And Gareth? Her lips quirked wryly. He seemed determined too! He was even ready to go so far as to offer—no, *that* wasn't the right word—to *accomplish* marriage to achieve her. *He must really be getting desperate,* she mused. *I'm sure marriage was the last thing he ever calculated on.*

And there lay the crux of her problem. In spite of her words to her mother, Morgain had not really given serious thought to marriage with Gareth. Or marriage to anyone, she admitted with total honesty. She enjoyed her job immensely and her independence even more. Marriage was serious, and she had always known that for her it would entail a depth of commitment that would wrench her life into new directions.

She had strong convictions about marriage. If she ever committed herself body and soul to someone, she was prepared for it to be for life. Marriages had to be built, day by day, but when she made her vows to the man who stood beside her she would mean every word and would expect nothing less of him. For richer, for poorer. In sickness and in health. And cleaving *only* one to another. Morgain was not a halfway person.

She was a realist. Gareth was certainly neither saint nor celibate monk. His eyes and deft, experienced hands told her that! But she was not concerned with what had gone before. It was the man as he was now, today, that she would take and to whom she would make her vows, the man he would be in the days of their lives together. He was the man into whose hands she would entrust her happiness and peace of mind and who could destroy her with the power she would therefore give him.

To love was to be vulnerable, and although she loved Gareth now, she realized that her love would deepen and grow through the years, fed by shared experience. If she cut Gareth out of her life now, she would bleed and it would leave a deep scar, but if she had to do it after marriage it could, no, would, destroy her. If she gave her trust to Gareth and he betrayed her, he would kill her as surely as though he stabbed her with a knife. Not physically, but as a person, embittering her and twisting her nature beyond repair.

I'm afraid, she realized with surprise. *I don't really trust Gareth and I'm afraid of the power he already holds over me. I know he wants me, would even marry me to get me, but for how long? I don't really know how he feels about me beyond desiring me. Is he capable of the depth of commitment I need? We fight, we spar for dominance, but does he realize that if one of us wins, we both lose?*

She gnashed her teeth in frustration. So many questions

150

and not one damned answer! With a groan she turned face down into her pillow.

Gareth, in his hotel suite, was having no greater success in finding ease of mind. His invective as he drove back to the hotel had been audible and scorching. Frustration tinged with bewilderment sent him scowling up the service stairs two at a time after he reached the hotel. He needed release through physical exertion, and that release could hardly be obtained by punching the elevator button through the other side of the wall. He stormed into his suite and slammed the door.

· Morgain was going to drive him insane! His ring was on her finger. She had lain pliant and yielding in his arms and right now, if she stood before him, he might *strangle* her slowly with the greatest satisfaction, after, of course, throwing her on the bed and making love to that lovely body until it moaned and writhed with pleasure beneath him.

He had just taken a mouthful of Scotch when the thought of Morgain submissive and eager in his arms burned its heady vision into his mind. The involuntary gasp and subsequent coughing fit distracted him only slightly from his thoughts of mayhem.

"Blast her," he choked weakly to the empty room. "She's dangerous to me even when she's miles away."

He finished the dregs of the liquid in his glass more warily and cradled it absently, rolling it between his palms while he stared out of the window, not really seeing the romantically lit grounds of the hotel's garden and swimming pool. Gradually most of the mingled rage and frustrated passion drained away, leaving him feeling spent and weary.

Two weeks ago, he thought incredulously, *I didn't know*

she existed. Now she fills my thoughts and twists my guts in knots. I've had to trick a ring on her finger because I was afraid to ask her outright to marry me. She might have said no. And if she'd said no? the voice in his mind questioned him slyly.

"She's mine!" he snarled aloud to the empty room. "She belongs to me and I'll break her neck if she so much as looks at another man." There was nothing either remotely melodramatic or absurd in his manner as he paced and spoke aloud to the quivering air. He intended to be the man in possession!

He was discovering that where Morgain was concerned, he had a capacity, even a compulsion, for possessiveness. He wanted all of Morgain's thoughts and desires to be to him. He would fill her mind as she filled his, driving out all thoughts of other men, other relationships. She was *his* woman, and he'd see to it that she remained so for the rest of their lives.

He no longer needed the cold shower. All of the pent-up energy he had been unable to release in passion was now channeled, directed toward achieving the most important goal he had ever aimed for in his life. Failure would render all other goals ashes on his tongue. A smile stretched his mouth. He wouldn't fail. "Morgain, my darling hellcat," he sent the thought winging to her miles away, "prepare to be married."

He made his plans and then slept, a smile curling the edges of his lips.

The next morning Morgain rose, heavy-eyed and unrefreshed. Nothing was resolved, and for the first time in her life she dreaded going to work. She wanted nothing more than to be able to burrow back down into her pillow and

152

escape the inevitable questions, questions for which she had no answers. By now word of the happenings at the hotel would have spread with brush-fire rapidity, and even though her parents had tactfully been abed when she came home last night, she didn't deceive herself that they hadn't heard, and having heard, would not expect her to flesh out the skeleton of rumor with warm fact.

The ring rode easily on her finger, scintillating as her hands moved about their accustomed tasks of dressing and making her sadly rumpled bed, a mute testament to her uneasy night. She considered taking it off again but knew that she would not. The next time she removed it would be either when she gave it back to Gareth for good or when it came off temporarily to make room for a wedding band. The time for half measures, not that those would ever serve with Gareth anyway, were gone. Events were rushing toward resolution, and she felt woefully unprepared.

When she walked into the kitchen, her parents looked up from their coffee cups. Her surmise was proved all too accurate when she saw that both of their gazes went immediately to her left hand. With a wry grin she held out the hand, palm down, for inspection.

Her father's keen gaze lifted to her face and noted the tired shadows under her blue eyes, the tension-tightness around the mouth. Definitely not the glowing radiance of a happy bride-to-be. Miri had noted all this as well, and a small, worried line drew itself between her brows. She poured, sugared liberally, and milked a large cup of coffee.

"So you and Gareth are engaged?" Miri's quiet query was accompanied by gentle pressure as she placed the cup in Morgain's hands.

"So it would seem," responded Morgain, her tone neutral. A faint smile quirked the mobile lips. "Who got in

153

with the news first, Mabel Gordon or Sylvia Harwell? They both rushed out of the hotel dining room like reporters with the scoop of the year yelling 'Stop the presses!' after they had stopped by to ask after you and Dad while we were having dinner."

Miri grinned. "Sylvia beat Mabel by five minutes, but then Mable lives farther out in the country and I guess it took her longer to get home." She hesitated and then continued. "I gather Gareth outmaneuvered Eric?"

Morgain shook her head in reluctant admiration. "Eric never had a chance. The ring was on my finger before Eric even opened his mouth. We won't go into how Gareth knew who Eric was and that he was engaged to Cathy, right now"—she shot a glance at her father, who had the grace to look slightly abashed—"because things had to come to a head sooner or later." She sighed. "I just didn't expect it to be *this* soon!"

She sipped broodingly at her coffee while her parents' eyes met in silent communion above her down-bent head. The silent messages flew back and forth. Miri spoke into the small silence, going directly to the heart of the matter. "Are you going to marry him?"

"I don't know." Morgain didn't lift her eyes from contemplation of the coffee remaining in her cup. "I don't know what Gareth really intends, what he means by this ring, and until I do . . ." She finished with a shrug and drank again.

Daniel's face darkened. "You don't mean you think he's using the offer of marriage to . . . to . . ." he sputtered, unable to complete the sentence.

"To get into bed with me?" Morgain finished calmly. "Yes, I'm sure he is." She looked up at her father and grinned ever so slightly. "Why not? I'd like to go to bed

154

with him," she said frankly, and watched her father blush a deep red. She also heard her mother make a smothered, choking snicker but didn't take her eyes from her father's face. *That, Father dear, was for Eric and Cathy,* she thought silently, and continued aloud, laying a placating hand on his clenched fist.

"Now Dad, I've always been able to speak frankly to you. You've always told Ken and me never to be embarrassed about anything we had to say to you."

"Well, I never quite envisioned having my daughter tell me that she fancied going to bed with a man with such devastating bluntness," said Daniel, recovering gamely. "You're woman-grown now, but a man's attitude toward his daughter generally freezes his inward vision of her at about six years of age." Daniel came strongly back to the point. "Do you really feel that Gareth asked you to marry him solely as a means of getting you to go to bed with him?"

Morgain relaxed back in her chair, and her mouth lifted in a wry grin. She lifted one finger to tick off a point. "First, he's never asked me to marry him. Last night he just slid the ring on my finger and *voilà,* instant engagement. Second"—she lifted the adjoining finger—"I don't know whether he sees the engagement solely as a means of getting me to go to bed with him. And by that I think we mean two different things. I think you mean a little prewedding hanky-panky and poof, there goes the engagement, exit Gareth stage left. Yes?"

Daniel nodded slowly. Morgain shook her head in disagreement. "Oh, no. Gareth means to marry me. You can be sure of that." Daniel sagged back into his own chair, but Miri maintained her alertness. Womanlike, she understood Morgain's point and knew that here lay the heart of her dilemma.

Morgain continued earnestly. "You see, Dad, I don't know what Gareth means this marriage to be. If he sees it as merely legal sex, to be tidied away by lawyers when the thrill has gone, then I want no part of it. I can think of easier ways of committing emotional suicide, and while I might be able to get over it if I stopped seeing him *now,* I know that that kind of marriage would damage me beyond all mending. I'd rather have an affair with him, and you know what I've always thought about *that* sort of relationship, at least for myself. Maybe other people can handle it, but I'm afraid I'm not built that way.

"I think our main trouble, Gareth's and mine, is that we don't really know each other all that well. We've fought, but we haven't really talked. I don't know what he thinks about the really important things between two people, the fundamentals that build or break a relationship." She sighed and rose from the chair. "I love him, but I don't trust him . . . yet. When I can trust him, I'll marry him. If I find I can't, I'll give him back this ring."

She headed for the kitchen door, pausing momentarily as her mother said, "Morgain, your breakfast . . ."

"I'm not hungry, Mom. A missed meal now and then won't hurt me, and I'm going to be late as it is. See you all this evening."

While Morgain drove to work she considered her words to her parents. It was true she had always thought that women who indulged in casual affairs were trading the gold for the dross. Innately fastidious herself, Morgain could not conceive of giving herself to a man she did not love passionately and completely. Mature in many ways, she still tended to see only stark blacks and whites in the

156

area of sexual behavior as it touched her own life. All of her yea or nay decisions had been easy until now because she had never met a man who could stir her as Gareth had done.

She had to face it. Last night all of her high-sounding moral principles had vanished like a drop of water on a red-hot skillet, sizzled away by the fire he so easily kindled in her body. Last night she would have done anything he asked, had in fact *begged* for him to take her. Her face flamed again in the agony of his rejection.

But why? Suddenly she asked herself why, why had he not taken what she so insistently offered? He wanted her. *That* was unmistakable. Good Lord, he was even going to *marry* her to get her! Morgain's thoughts chased each other like rats on a treadmill all the way to work. She knew instinctively that last night held the key to her questions and it was vital that she correctly interpret what that incident could tell her.

She was still deep in her mental musings when she parked the car at the airfield and entered the office. John and Ken were at the coffeepot, pouring cups of the vile black brew the long unscoured pot produced. Ken automatically filled a cup for Morgain.

Morgain grasped the handle with her left hand while her right went out to lift the sugar holder. Ken caught the flash of the ring . . . it was, after all, too big to miss . . . and his hand shot out to grasp her wrist. The coffee sloshed, and they both yelped as the steaming droplets stung on bare skin. Morgain set the cup back on the counter and sucked the back of her hand where reddened spots had appeared.

John had watched this bit of byplay safely out of range of the flying liquid, but now he stepped forward and point-

157

ed a questioning fingertip at her ring finger, eyebrows raised in interrogative arcs.

"Yes, it's Gareth's," Morgain affirmed, her words somewhat muffled against the back of her hand.

Ken whistled a low, sustained tone and grinned. "Boy, did Jenny fall down on the job! I count on her to tell me all the news, fit to print or not, and she hasn't even heard that my own sister is engaged. Are we invited to the wedding, Morgain?"

"Of course, Ken," said a smooth deep voice at her shoulder. Morgain jumped involuntarily. "What did you do to your hand, darling?" questioned that same voice as an irresistible hand pulled her injured one away from her lips, so that two keen green eyes could ascertain the damage. The reddened splotches were already fading, but Gareth lifted the hand to his mouth and pressed a kiss to each mark. "Kiss it and make it better, sweetheart?" he murmured quietly.

Morgain looked at him sharply but instead of the ironic glints she expected to encounter, she could only see herself, reflected and trapped in the inscrutable depths of his eyes. Her ring had slid forward toward the knuckle and she felt his thumb gently but firmly ease it back into position, and then run caressingly up and down the length of that finger. Her heart started to hammer and she tried unobtrusively to regain possession of her hand, but he would not let go. *The story of my life recently,* she thought acidly. *The more I try to wiggle loose, the harder it is to get away from him.*

John and Ken moved away from the couple, heavily tactful, but neither Gareth nor Morgain noticed their absence. They were once again locked in silent communion, oblivious to outer influences. Morgain found that the echoes of last night's passion had not died away, and to judge by Gareth's hungry, possessive gaze, he was finding the same.

His hand came up from his side, and as a blind man might, with tentative fingers he traced the rise of her cheekbones, softly, gently, past her temple and so to the back of her head. The gentle pressure pulled her toward him almost imperceptibly, and at the same time tilted her head back, lifting her face up, positioning it for his seeking lips. As though lead-weighted, Morgain's eyelids drooped, slipping downward to hide the sight of his descending face.

He tasted the sigh that ghosted from her lips just as his mouth closed over her slightly parted mouth, and the kiss that he had meant to be a gentle greeting somehow got out of hand. He could not stop himself from drinking deeply, a man ending a centuries-long drought. This woman was his oasis in the desert, the fountain of all delight, and he meant his kiss to tell her so.

Just at that moment Morgain would have been incapable of reading a message written in letters ten feet high and plastered on a billboard. The fire she had thought put out by tears last night was blazing wildly through her body, consuming intentions and resolutions as if they had never been made. She was helpless in the grip of her desire for him, and with a desperate moan she arched her body into his, fitting every curve and hard outline with precision.

Reality intruded with prosaic abruptness when the outer door of the office flew open and one of the men who helped to stow the cargo in the planes stuck his head in and yelled, "Hey, John, isn't anyone going to come out and supervise the cargo loading? Tony and I've been wait-

159

ing for a half an hour, and I've got to leave for Barnwell's in forty minutes to pick up their consignment."

Morgain went rigid in Gareth's arms and then sagged weakly against him again, burying her hot face in his chest. Zeb, his eye drawn by the movement, spotted them and stammered, "Oh . . . um . . . hi, Morgain. Mr. Hammond."

Before Gareth could reply—Morgain was incapable of forming a coherent word, and besides her face was still thrust firmly into the front of his shirt—John and Ken came out of the inner office where they had tactfully retreated. Ken shot the entwined couple a speculative glance, opened his mouth, primed to tease Morgain a little, and caught Gareth's eye. He swallowed the words hastily and followed John and the staring Zeb out the door.

Morgain was muttering into his chest, and Gareth held her away slightly so he could hear her clearly.

"Damn, damn, damn!" He wondered if her maledictions were falling on the unfortunate Zeb's head or his own, but when she lifted her eyes to his, he realized she meant them for herself. "What are you doing to me, Gareth? I . . . I . . ." She pulled back out of his arms and lifted shaking hands between them. "Look at me. I'm not fit to fly!" She watched the fine tremors in her hands with wonderment. "Even after we missed a midair by fifteen feet six months ago my hands didn't shake like this. You devastate me, Gareth, and I don't think I can handle it. Please, please let me go. I'm out of my league. Let me go."

"No!" He grasped her hands and pulled her roughly back into his arms. "I can't, Morgain. I won't. Trust me. I won't hurt you, sweetheart."

"Can I trust you, Gareth?" She looked up at him soberly, eyes glistening brightly, unshed tears brimming but not spilling. "You could destroy me, you know, and it's hard to trust someone who has that power over you."

He stiffened, listening for the meaning that lay beneath her words. Trust was part of love, and she did not trust him. If she came to trust him, would she then admit she loved him? And destruction? The power to devastate and destroy her. Love gave that power. He knew that full well because when he had admitted to himself that he loved her, he had passed that power into her hands. She could use this burning, raging love he felt for her to crush him like an ant if she chose, but he knew she would not. He trusted her.

Would words serve? He could assure her of his love, promise her his devotion and fidelity, but words were glib, and though he had never used promises, either spoken or implied, to get what he wanted from women, Morgain could not know that. He'd had no love nor words of love for the women who had passed through his life before, but would the words fall fresh and new-minted on her ears when there was no trust?

Gareth held her tightly, inescapably, and Morgain stood quietly, her momentary flutter of rebellion spent. *Speak to me, Gareth*, she thought. *Tell me what you're thinking, what you're feeling. Let me into your mind with words. I mistrust my body and your body and the messages they exchange.*

"Morgain," he began slowly, and her eyes flamed with hope. The door banged again as John and Ken tromped back inside. She could have screamed.

"I do believe they've turned into pillars of salt, John," Ken jested jocularly. Blue and green eyes glared at him, and he ostentatiously turned up his nonexistent overcoat

161

collar. "Brr, the temperature just dropped 120°. D'you think it'll snow this afternoon?"

"For a man of your age you have a strangely sophomoric sense of humor, Ken," was Morgain's crushing response to her brother's teasing.

"Aargh!" Ken staggered back dramatically, clutching his chest. "Straight through the heart. Gareth, are you sure you know what you're doing? She has a tongue like a stiletto and a wicked right hook."

Gareth grinned. "Oh, yes, I know what I'm doing." He bent and dropped a kiss on the tip of her nose. "I know what I'm doing, and why." The last words reached only Morgain's ears and her eyes searched his face.

"Why?" It was the merest whisper, but it carried an urgency that was unmistakable.

A look of such tenderness came into his face that Morgain felt her knees might buckle. She had never seen such a look on Gareth's, or any man's, face before. It was like coming in from a snowstorm and being wrapped in a big warmed woolly blanket, knowing that you are safe and warm again, cherished and cuddled. *Now,* she thought. *Now he'll tell me and then I'll know. He'll say the words I need to hear and I won't have to wonder and doubt and fear.*

But she had forgotten the outside world again, and while neither Ken nor John were particularly insensitive, neither were they blessed with much delicacy.

John, with an eye to his schedules, grumbled, "Well, congratulations, you two, and now let's get on with it. Ken, you're loaded and clear to go. Morgain, the Buckeye load will be stowed in fifteen minutes. Weather reports are on my desk, and when you've checked them, see me about the rest of the schedule. I want you to divert over to

162

Torbert on your way back to pick up a small load he has. I told him we'd be by for it today. Gareth, are you going up to Buckeye with Morgain? We'll be hauling a full load, and if you want the space, something will have to come out.

"No, John," Gareth responded easily, but his eyes were rueful as he looked at Morgain. "I just came to say good morning to my fiancée. I have to go to Los Angeles today and I'll be gone several days. Buck Stevens is coming in to pick me up in two hours, and I wanted to see Morgain before I left. I didn't get a chance last night to tell her that I was leaving. There were other things more urgent."

A strange mixture of emotions swirled in Morgain. Disappointment, frustration, curiosity, and more . . . all struggling for expression. "When will you be back?" she queried Gareth, low-voiced and hesitant.

"I'm not sure, exactly, sweetheart." Her eyes flashed up to his face at the unaccustomed endearment, and he smiled down at her, his eyes seeking to send her a message she wasn't sure she could read or believe. "I'll be back by the weekend, and Morgain"—he laid a hand along her neck, his thumb stroking her cheek—"we'll talk, uninterrupted, when I get back, hmm?"

"Yes, I think it's time we talked," she agreed soberly. "We never have, you know. We've fought and argued and . . ." Her voice trailed off as she saw where her sentence was leading.

Gareth was no gentleman. He laughed. "Yes, we certainly have, haven't we?" he chuckled, and gave her a purely wicked smile.

"Gareth!" Her tone was scandalized and stiff. Her blue eyes began to spit sparks, and he thought again how lovely she was, even when she was preparing to jump on him with both feet.

"Whoa! Pax! Peace! Send me off with a kiss, not a kick, my little spitfire. I'll be gone for several days," he informed her whimsically. "Give me something sweet to sustain me while I'm gone."

Her eyes narrowed. *'Something sweet, you . . . you . . . MAN!* she thought. *I'll blow out every one of your circuits!* Aloud she said, "Of course, Gareth darling. I'll give you something to keep you warm." She glided up very close to him and wound her arms around his neck, pulling his mouth down to meet her lips before he had time to brace himself.

If smoke didn't shoot out of his ears, it wasn't for lack of heat generated. He had taught her a lot in the short time they had known each other, and she had a strong natural talent. For once in his life the initiative was out of his hands, and Gareth found it an unnerving experience, which was just what Morgain had done her best to insure. She was determined to give him something to remember while he was in the wild and wayward big city, and the kiss, as kisses go, rated high on the Richter scale. When she backed away from him, Gareth didn't try to hold her, and his eyes were slightly unfocused. He was also breathing raggedly.

"Have a good trip, darling," she purred in feline content. "Give me a call when you get back into town." She walked to the door of the inner office, adding a deliberate touch of "something extra" to the sway of her hips. She gave him one last, languishing glance before she went in. The glimpse she got of his face before she shut the door between them was balm to her jangled nerves. A poleax couldn't have done a better job, she considered with satisfaction. There are times when it is necessary to fight fire with fire and if Gareth got a bit scorched around the edges, tough!

She realized that her hands were no longer shaking, but her knees seemed to have a disconcerting tendency to want to bend backward, or something. This guerrilla warfare was going to make a nervous wreck of her, and she was glad that Gareth was going to go away. If she had any more emotional scenes today, she'd have to turn in her Class I FAA physical certificate because her blood pressure would break the gauge on the blood pressure cuff. She'd only been awake a little more than an hour and a half and already she felt as wrung out as she had after she'd flown through that storm on the mercy mission to Buckeye. Gareth was not a restful person.

CHAPTER VII

Morgain heard nothing from Gareth while he was gone. At first she was pleased. She had welcomed the chance to regain her equilibrium, free from Gareth's disturbing presence. It took her a day and a half to start missing him. In fact, she was on the return leg of a Buckeye run when the day suddenly went flat.

The first day, the day Gareth left, went well and swiftly. After her initially shaky start Morgain made all of her scheduled flights, buoyed by a dual sense of freedom. The sky was hers in a way that none but those who fly can understand. Gareth was gone, and for a time she would have to fight neither him nor her own desires. She was free, and had she not been ferrying delicate electronic equipment going and a shaky-stomached passenger back, she would have stunted the plane across the sky.

The second day began well too. She woke from the best sleep she'd had in days, after a peaceful evening spent washing her hair, listening to music, and curling up with a good book. She spoke civilly to John and Ken and whistled while she preflighted her assigned airplane. The two men shot each other significant glances. They presumed she was a woman in love, subject to whims and fancies, but who were they to cavil at such sunny weather?

There were, of course, all the sayings about the course of true love never running smoothly, but in the opinions of John and Ken, Morgain and Gareth had carried those old sayings to the extreme!

At Buckeye, Morgain had a cup of coffee with Charley, stopped in to see the man whose life her mercy mission had saved, and took off from the runway with the same lifted spirits her entrance into the world of the air always gave her. The even drone of the engine was singing in her ears; the response of the controls made the plane an extension of her body. She was a happy woman.

The malaise descended on her spirit without warning. She had been contemplating her schedule for the evening, mapping out her activities, when she realized that since she wouldn't see Gareth tonight, nothing was appealing. The book she had been reading with such enjoyment was boring and ill-written, current television programs had been expressly designed for the mentally deficient, and the formerly sunny and cloudless blue sky was inexplicably dimmed and lusterless. In fact, she was blackly depressed.

By the time she got back to base, she was fuming, furious with herself for being such an idiot. It was like being addicted to some drug, and the withdrawal symptoms were excruciating. Insidiously this craving for the sight and, yes, damn it, the touch of Gareth had crept up on her, and the weekend, when he had promised to return, was an aeon away.

It was really ludicrous. She was mooning over him like a subteen in the first throes of puppy love. If she hadn't felt so absolutely rotten, Morgain would have laughed herself silly. But she didn't feel at all like laughing, so she did the next best thing. She bit John's head off when he made some joking comment about young lovers. John muttered something about "I knew it was too peaceful around here" and disappeared into his office.

Morgain went home.

By the time the weekend neared, more people than Morgain were eager for Gareth to return. Love was not having a beatific effect on her. She was racked by doubt, of both herself and Gareth, and the resultant inner turmoil affected everything but her actual flying. Sometimes her mood had all the charm of a she-bear with a festered thorn in her paw, and sometimes she was reasonably human. The catch, her friends and family discovered, was to know which mood was upon her at any given time. Consequently, mealtimes were full of pregnant silences and sidelong looks.

Miri counseled patience when Daniel's was all but exhausted, reminding him that his own father had threatened him with the woodshed at the ripe age of twenty-four while they were courting, after one of their more notable tiffs. Daniel subsided, but Miri considered that it had been a near thing. She resolved to take head firmly in hand and speak to Morgain herself, but Morgain, repentant, forestalled her and apologized to both her parents.

"I'm sorry, Mom and Dad. There was no excuse for taking my foul temper out on you two. I don't know what's come over me the last few days." She grimaced and amended hastily before Daniel could enlighten her. "Well, yes, I do know what's come over me, but I never expected it to strike me quite this way." She continued with a rather bitter twist to her shapely mouth. "The poets must have rocks in their heads. If love gives everyone such a hard time, the human race has much more staying power than I ever gave it credit for having. It should have become extinct a long time ago."

Daniel shuffled mentally through his stock of soothing platitudes but found none that would do the slightest bit of good. He didn't know what was going to happen when Gareth and Morgain finally met again this weekend, but anything was better than what he had been enduring. After sitting precariously upon a barrel of slow-burning gunpowder for a while, the resultant explosion almost comes as a relief.

Morgain could have seconded his thoughts had she been privy to them. She had mentally renounced Gareth so many times during internal debates between her head and her heart that she was exhausted, and was coming to view the pending encounter with something approaching dull resignation.

She knew now that never to see Gareth again would be to cut the heart out of her body, and she feared the coming confrontation with an uncharacteristic cowardice. What if she had read those tiny signs and portents wrongly? Could a man such as she believed him to be truly become the type of man necessary for their mutual felicity? She *must* have a tender lover, a staunch companion, a man for all seasons, and she would be thus to him.

She had no illusions about her own makeup. Hers was no saintly, forgiving spirit. Betrayal would unleash the worst side of her nature. She would love with a whole heart, but the other side of the coin was there, face down. She could hate with a whole heart as well . . . the potential was implicit, seeds of her and his destruction, and she would rather, in truth, cut out her own heart than ever see them flower.

She loved Gareth. She knew and accepted that, loved him so much that she would give him up if she could not be absolutely sure of him, lest at some future date she destroy them both. There were other obstacles as well, and when she considered the list, her spirit quailed.

She loved flying. It was a part of her, and her job was challenging. She looked forward to moving up in rank and someday wearing the four stripes of a captain. But somehow she could not see Gareth with a working wife nor, if she were honest with herself, was she sure she could abide the separations her job would entail. But on the other hand she was no hausfrau, content to bake and clean her days away, waiting for the lord and master to return to a spotless castle.

And children. The thought of bearing Gareth's children lit a sensual fire deep within her body, but would either of them make good parents? He had held newborn Jeremy with unflustered ease, but a sweet-smelling, sleeping infant is an entirely different animal from a smelly, yowling one at two o'clock in the morning. Would he? And would she? And when the decision was reached, would their decisions be in accord?

Round and round the same weary track the questions trudged, nose to tail tip. She could not seem to halt their ceaseless plodding. In her heart she knew no answers would come until Gareth came, but to *tell* oneself a thing is not the same as being able to *listen* to what is being told.

It could not be said that she pined. She was no delicate flower to droop and fade, but the signs of strain were there. Faint shadows beneath the eyes, a tension in the set and swing of her shoulders, a finely drawn sculpture of skin over bone in the face that spoke mutely of some weight loss.

She was splendidly healthy. The excess consumption of coffee and picked-over meals from loss of appetite would not quickly undermine her basic health, but Miri watched her with troubled eyes and dreaded what would come should Morgain and Gareth be unable to resolve their differences. She knew Morgain's stubborn will, and knew too that she would be capable of making and holding to a decision to refuse Gareth if she really came to the conclusion that their ways did not lie together. She could see, too, the foretaste of the price Morgain would pay for such a decision.

Saturday came at last, and none too soon for all. Morgain spent a restless night, tossing from dreams both sensual and troubled, and the gray-cast skies did nothing to quiet her spirit. What if the weather went out of minimums again and Gareth could not fly in? Another day of conversation with herself and she would indeed begin to talk to herself, but aloud this time. She might even gibber a bit. So much for the calm and collected professional image.

She dressed in shorts and shirt (but they were new and very flattering) and her hair was silky clean. The skin beneath the clothes had been bathed and lotioned and powdered, and if some of the hoarded perfume, souvenir of a trip to England and France the summer before, had been dabbed here and there, only the nose knew for sure. Daniel's nose twitched when she entered the kitchen and crossed to the window to look out, but he was a smart father and an even smarter man. He complimented neither her looks nor her fragrance.

"I thought the weather was going to be a repeat of last weekend," he commented, perhaps a trifle unwisely. He saw Miri wince, and he hastened to add, "but I see it's clearing nicely. I guess I'll have to cut the grass after all."

His falsely lugubrious air brought a smile to both Miri's and Morgain's faces because there was nothing Daniel enjoyed more than working in the yard. His efforts kept both his own household and Ken's well supplied with produce and fresh flowers, to the considerable benefit of their grocery bills, not to mention their palates. For weeks after she had been home on a visit Morgain could hardly endure the pseudovegetables of the inflight meals the crew was served. Of course, the taste buds eventually readjusted to what was available, but it was never a pleasant process.

Contrary to her habit of the past few days, Morgain ate an enormous breakfast: scrambled eggs, sausage, toast and jelly. Daniel watched with awe and Miri with satisfaction. Morgain leaned back in her chair and sipped at her second cup of coffee.

"My, that was a good breakfast, Mom. You're the only person I know who can cook scrambled eggs just right every time . . . not too dry and not too runny. Compliments to the chef." She picked up the last sausage and nibbled on it reflectively. It's a wonder to me that Dad doesn't weigh 350 pounds by now."

Daniel slapped a midriff that would not have disgraced a man twenty-five years younger and leered at his wife. "She works it off of me. She may be a fantastic cook, but she's also a slave driver. It's a wonder I'm not a shadow of my former self by now."

"Who was your former self, Dad?" Morgain queried with interest. "I never knew you believed in reincarnation."

She ducked as Daniel took a playful swipe at her, and shook her head sadly. "His reflexes are going too. You'd better trade him in on a newer model, Mom."

"My reflexes are still good enough to turn you over my knee, brat," promised her father as he advanced purposefully toward her.

"Child abuse, child abuse," shrieked Morgain as she ducked behind her mother. She made spectacles of her fingers circling her eyes and peered at him over her mother's shoulder. "You wouldn't hit a person wearing glasses, would you?" she entreated pathetically.

"With pleasure," growled Daniel as he lunged. Morgain pushed her laughing mother into his arms and ran lightly to the back door.

"Sorry to sacrifice you, Mother, but it's every man for himself."

Daniel, being otherwise occupied, ceased his pursuit.

Without reason Morgain was suddenly lighthearted. The waiting time was over, and she knew Gareth would come today. He had promised. Even had the weather not cooperated, somehow he would come. She knew with a certainty she could not have explained in rational terms. Nothing was solved yet, but for the moment she was tranquil. All the frets and fevers of the last few days melted away, ephemeral snowflakes that no longer chilled her.

She helped in Daniel's garden, weeding with such a will that several rows of carrots had an unscheduled thinning. He said not a word. She could have uprooted the whole garden without a comment from him, so pleased was he to see a genuine smile on her face.

Gareth found her, directed there by Miri, when he arrived in the early afternoon. He stood for a long, quiet minute, watching the grace of her figure as she bent and twisted. He saw her lips move as she tugged at a recalcitrant weed and, knowing his lady love, was sure it was better uttered sotto voce.

Gone was the tidy, scrubbed young woman of the morning. The face she lifted was dirt-streaked and sweaty, but the smile that illuminated her face when she saw him approaching had the wattage of a lighthouse searchlight. She sprang to her feet and came to his opened arms with the candid instinct of a child.

It was not a child's kiss they exchanged, however. Gareth had carried the memory of Morgain's "good journey" kiss with him, a talisman, though he knew at the time that she had given it to him with no pure intent. With a sensitivity to her thoughts she would not have credited, he knew she had meant the kiss as a charm, to ward off the wiles of other women while he was away from her. It had been a measure of her inability to trust him fully, as one day she must. This kiss carried just as much voltage, but it was sheer welcome. When they broke for breath, he murmured raggedly in her ear, "Kiss me like that again and I'll be forced to ravish you amid the radishes."

Unabashed, Morgain shot back, "Is that from the same song as 'Tiptoe Through the Tulips'? She bit him delicately on the upper chest and finished, "Perhaps from the unexpurgated version?"

He laughed with full-bodied enjoyment and hugged her breathless. Then he released her to cup his hands around her face, looking down seriously into the wide blue eyes. "I've missed you, darling. I've grudged every minute I had to be apart from you."

Her eyelashes veiled her eyes for a flickering instant and then lifted. The time for evasions was past. Morgain knew that from now on everything must be unambiguous and frank. She would not hide behind pride or fear of exposing her deepest feelings. If she and Gareth were to have a future, only the truth between them would serve.

"I've missed you the same way, Gareth. All of my friends and relatives will testify to that. They all bear the claw marks of my abominable bad temper, which has been notable for its persistence and intensity since you left. I think I may have given John a permanent tic in his left eye. Yesterday he wondered if it was possible to fly with one's leg in a cast after all."

He grinned at her, triumph leaping in his eyes. "I left a few twitching bodies behind me myself. It'll take my L.A. operation some time to recover, I'm afraid."

He dropped a quick kiss on her mouth, slid his hands caressingly down the sides of her neck to her shoulders, and turned her to face the house. He propelled her toward the back door, hands firmly guiding, brooking no deviations from the course he set.

"Go get cleaned up and changed, Morgain, darling." She shot a look back over her shoulder where he loomed behind her, keeping pace. "Please," he added in tacit acknowledgment of the sparks that were beginning to arc in her eyes.

"Of course, Gareth," she said sweetly. "I'm always willing to go along with any reasonable *request*," she emphasized.

He registered the hit with a chuckle, but his hands didn't ease their gentle persistence until she mounted the steps to the kitchen door. He reached around her, opened the door, and ushered her inside.

"I'll let your mother know you won't be here for dinner." He pulled her to him, pressing her close up and down the length of his hard body, his hands cupping the firm curve of her buttocks. She gasped and arched into him with involuntary hunger and met his famished kiss with the unsated appetite of her own. With that kiss she made him a promise, inevitable and inescapable.

* * *

176

The dress she chose was a silky slither of blues and greens, thin-strapped and held in place mainly by the elastic that banded it around the top. It had one button in the back, where the elastic met, and fell open to the waist where another button closed the skirt at the top of a short zipper. She had bought it during a temporary aberration, loving the feel and look of the dress, but had never dared to wear it on any date. It was enticement, impure and simple, and the tantalizing glimpse of spine was uninterrupted by bra or slip.

She piled her hair atop her head, securing it with one decorative comb. One comb was easier to keep track of than a bunch of hairpins. A few tendrils, curling softly from the moisture of the shower, escaped the comb's confinement, but she left them. No jewelry but *the* ring. Not *her* ring yet, but after tonight . . .

She found Gareth sitting with her parents on the front porch, sipping at an ice-filled fresh fruit drink. He rose and put a proprietorial arm around her waist, and they stood together facing her parents.

Symbolic perhaps, but all at once Miri felt her fears for Morgain's happiness fade away. There was something so right in the look of the couple standing before them. . . . She glanced at Daniel, and their own private communication told her he sensed it too. They watched Gareth escort Morgain to his car, and Miri noted with womanly amusement that Gareth's thumb could not resist the lure of that inviting glimpse of Morgain's back. His hand rode at the back of her waist and his thumb was even now investigating her silky spine. *I think the war's about over* was her final thought as she and Daniel went back in the house.

Gareth didn't start the car immediately. He sat for a

moment, merely looking over at her. "I like your dress," he said huskily. "It's a new one, I hope?"

"Why, no," Morgain replied innocently, "I've had it for some time, actually." He scowled. She laughed and relented. "But I've never worn it since the day I bought it." She wrinkled her nose impudently at him. "I didn't dare."

"I don't wonder," he retorted. "It needs an overcoat of barbed wire held together with a 'NO TRESPASSING' sign to make it safe for public consumption." Before she could make a comment in response, he continued, "It's a good thing I don't plan to put you on public view tonight."

She couldn't resist the dig. "Are you a prude, Gareth, darling?"

"No, you little witch. You know damn well what I mean. I don't want other men looking at you like—"

"Like you look at me?" she finished for him.

"Exactly!" he said forcefully, and started the car. She smothered a snicker, and he grinned over at her. "Morgain, if you live to a ripe old age it won't be your fault," he informed her.

Impenitent to the last she quoted, "A short life but a merry one."

She could feel Gareth observing her closely as he parked the car in the hotel parking lot. It was much too early for dinner, and she knew they weren't going to sit around drinking at the bar. She kept her face calmly composed, but her pulse rate would have given the lie to her calm façade had anyone taken it.

The elevator was empty. Gareth took the opportunity to run a questing finger the length of her spine from button to button. She quivered, and he said, "Definitely not for public consumption." She didn't answer him; her mouth was suddenly dry and she was having trouble swallowing.

178

She had thought out her battle plan, as it were, but it might be harder to stick to than she had expected. All too soon the elevator stopped and they were in the corridor leading to his suite. His hand on her elbow stopped her before a numbered door, and he inserted his key.

The living room was impersonally but tastefully decorated, with surprisingly attractive prints hung on the portion of the walls that was not taken up by the large window overlooking the hotel garden and the door that she knew must lead to the bedroom. All at once she could swallow freely. She was committed. She experienced a deep relief. The waiting time was indeed over, and the tomorrows could take care of themselves. For now she had the present.

She watched Gareth shoot the dead bolt on the outer door with calm eyes, and when he lifted the phone to inform the operator that he wanted no calls until further notice, she tossed her purse on the couch and kicked off her sandals.

When he had replaced the phone, he said, "Well, unless the hotel catches fire we should be safe from interruptions."

He turned back to face her and discovered that she was only a foot away. A half step more and she was in his arms. She matched him kiss for kiss, and suddenly he realized that his shirt was open to the waist and her hands were playing seductive music up and down his own bare spine.

"Morgain, stop that," he groaned as she nibbled on the skin over his collarbone. "I didn't bring you up here to seduce you, darling. I want to talk to you without fear of interruption." He tried to unwind her arms from around his neck, but she clung like a barnacle.

She tilted her head back, abandoning his collarbone for

179

the moment, and smiled mysteriously up at him. "Ah, but perhaps I came up here to seduce *you!*"

He looked down at her in stunned disbelief. "Have you been drinking, Morgain?" he questioned her suspiciously.

She snorted inelegantly. "Gareth Hammond, if this is a sample of your technique, let me inform you that your reputation as a rake must be shockingly overrated."

"Oh, Lord, sweetheart. You see before you no rake, just a thoroughly bewildered male."

"If you love me, you'll make love to me right now," she informed him.

"But we have to talk, Morgain," he insisted, holding on to his self-control with desperate but fast-failing good intentions.

"You can tell me what I want to know this way, my love," she assured him softly, and presented her back to him so that the buttons were within easy reach.

Good intentions died a quick death, but his fingers were shaky as he slipped the buttons open and ran the zipper down its short track. Morgain gave a lithe wriggle. The dress slithered smoothly down around her feet, leaving her clad only in silky, black lace bikini briefs. She stood before him, perfect in her innocent sensuality. The bruises on her shoulders were all gone, and there was not even a shadow remaining to mar the warm, gold texture of her skin. Even his fantasies hadn't been so devastatingly erotic!

Gareth tugged the comb from her hair and watched the glinting strands drop in a glorious, weighted, honey tumble to her shoulders. He buried one hand in its heavy depth, tilting her head up for his devouring kiss, while his other hand began to stroke the rich, full contours so tantalizingly displayed, circling and teasing her nipples with gentle fingers.

He picked her up as easily as he would lift a child and carried her into the bedroom, where he swept back the covers and placed her reverently on the bed. Before he came down to her he spoke with utmost sincerity. "Morgain, I love you. I have since that first day and I will past death. I've never said that to anyone else. I am your man and you are my woman. There are not, nor will there be, any others."

It was his pledge of fidelity, and all of her other questions receded to minor importance. Together they would solve their problems. With a smile of heart-shaking tenderness and love, she held wide her arms to receive him. She whispered, "I love you, my darling Gareth. You are my man. Make me your woman."

He was eager to obey. He moved to claim every throbbing inch of her. His hands, his lips, his tongue . . . with them he set the seal of his possession over her, from the rose-tipped heights of her passion-firmed breasts to the intimate depths of her most secret recesses. Lock and key, sword and sheath: with careful precision he joined them . . . two made one.

And so, at last, she understood fully the meaning of the words he had spoken in the car on the night he had given her her ring. With his body he paid homage to her feminine mystery, gifting her with a pleasure so exquisite that it overrode the nerve pathways, spiraling her down into the spasmodic insensibility of the little death. Then she was truly his woman, and she lay well content in the close comfort of his possessive embrace.

"Was it good for you, sweetheart?" he questioned her later, almost shyly, an anxious lover.

She answered him wordlessly, her kiss an accolade echoed and reinforced by the languorous satiation he could read on her face. He rolled over on his back, pulling her with him. She subsided against his chest, loving the feel of skin and hair, firm muscle and hard bone. She seemed inclined to drowse and dream, draped over him in the limber sprawl of total relaxation.

He stroked down her back idly, enjoying the tactile smooth sweep of skin. "Can we talk now?" he teased her.

She lifted her head and then bit him gently, sighing happily. "I suppose so, if you can't think of anything better to do."

He hugged her strongly. "Morgain, you are an unending delight . . . and wanton, too! I didn't ask you before. Will you marry me?"

"Yes, oh, yes, Gareth."

"Tomorrow?"

"Sure."

"Okay. How about two o'clock?"

She shot up out of his loose clasp and stared down at him in shock. "You're serious," she croaked.

He stretched, clasped his arms behind his head, and prepared to enjoy the delicious view. His smile was seraphic as he announced, "The church is arranged, we can tell your parents tonight, and the replacement pilot I brought back with me is installed here in the hotel, several floors below us. John can brief him tomorrow, and he'll start taking your flights on Monday. That gives us a week plus of your vacation for a honeymoon. Where would you like to spend it?"

When she didn't answer him, he nudged her and prompted her. "You're supposed to smile seductively at me and say, 'I'd like to spend it in bed.'"

"But my dress" was all she could offer weakly.

"In the closet. If it doesn't fit, I'll marry you without one. It'll save time," he leered.

She jumped off the bed and ran naked to the closet, tugging the door open. There, shrouded in plastic, hung a creamy white long dress. She turned back to face him, hands on hips.

"Well? Is two o'clock okay with you?" His attention wasn't really on her face, so she stamped her foot.

"Gareth Hammond," she began in dangerous accents. He watched her warily. "If it weren't for the fact that I want to marry you as much as you want to marry me, I'd tell you to go to hell." She ran back across the room and dove into his arms, laughing. "Don't think that you'll manage me so easily for the rest of our lives. It just so happens that you have an incredibly sexy body that I crave, but two can play at that game, you know." She wiggled enticingly against him, and he whooped with laughter. "Just you wait until I decide that there's something I want, you unscrupulous beast. Then we'll see who manages whom. I'll wind you around my little finger," she promised him.

His face was buried between her breasts, so his words were muffled. "It's not your finger I want to be wound around, you little hellcat, but you're welcome to try. Besides, I'm already three steps ahead of you. All I have to do is figure out what you want before you know yourself and then"—he kissed her and pulled her firmly back beneath his aroused body—"give it to you."

A long time later Gareth reopened communications with the outside world. Morgain waited in the bedroom until room service had come and gone, then she strolled out into the living room where dinner for two and champagne waited. So did Gareth.

She was wearing one of his shirts, sleeves rolled above the elbows, unbuttoned well past the cleavage line. Her long tanned legs were exposed from midthigh down. She smiled wickedly, "Are we dining formally tonight? Should I have put on a tie?"

"You should have put on an overcoat," he gritted as he assisted her into her chair. "It's not fair to test a man's self-control like this, and we are going to *talk.*"

"*Have* you any self-control?" she asked demurely.

"I haven't murdered you yet, have I?" he quashed her firmly.

He served her plate, poured her champagne, and as their glasses touched, the pledge their eyes made was life-binding. They ate silently for the most part, and when the dessert and coffee stage came, Gareth took her hand and absently began to slide the ring around on her finger. He seemed to be searching for words, and when he finally found them, the last of Morgain's doubts fled.

"How would you feel about changing your job, darling? I . . . uh . . . have an opening for a company pilot, and I can guarantee good working conditions." He didn't quite meet her eyes. He reminded her of a little boy offering a present he hopes his mother will really like. "I . . . we . . . that is, the company just bought a new Lear jet and . . ."

"A new Lear," she said faintly.

"Well," he said reasonably, "I have to travel quite a bit yet, and since I don't intend to leave you behind, I thought you might as well work for your keep. When we decide to have children we can hire an additional pilot and I'll arrange for someone else to do most of the traveling until we can both go again. By then we may be ready to settle down in one spot anyway. I have a house at Lake Tahoe

184

that I use mostly in the winter, and a couple of apartments, but we can base ourselves wherever you choose."

"Children? Are we having children?" She seemed to be unable to do more than stutter out incoherent questions. He had said they were going to talk, but her end of the conversation was less than scintillating.

He grinned. "A common result of activities such as we have recently indulged in, my love; but speaking of children in the abstract, yes, I think you and I could turn out a rather respectable specimen. I believe parenthood is an acquired art, and we're both good learners. So, *if* you will and *when* you will, sometime in the future, at our leisure . . . ?"

She began to laugh helplessly. "The war's over, Gareth. You've won. I surrender."

He scooped her into his arms and headed toward the bedroom again, leaving the coffee cooling in the cups behind them.

"If this is war, my darling, then it's the first one in history where every participant wins."

Breathtaking sagas
of adventure
and
romance

VALERIE
VAYLE

"THE MOST ROMANTIC NOVEL SINCE <u>LOVE STORY</u>"
—Good Housekeeping

Change of Heart

SALLY MANDEL

Once in a long while, a story is so bursting with charm and tenderness that its charm is irresistible.

That story is Sharlie and Brian's story, *Change of Heart*— a love story for a lifetime.

A Dell Book $2.95 (11355-5)

At your local bookstore or use this handy coupon for ordering:

Danielle Steel

**AMERICA'S
LEADING
LADY OF
ROMANCE
REIGNS
OVER ANOTHER BESTSELLER**

A Perfect Stranger

A flawless mix of glamour and love by
Danielle Steel, the bestselling author of
The Ring, Palomino and *Loving.*

A DELL BOOK $3.50   #17221-7

**VOLUME I
IN THE EPIC
NEW SERIES**

*The Morland
Dynasty*

The FOUNDING

by Cynthia Harrod-Eagles

THE FOUNDING, a panoramic saga rich with passion
and excitement, launches Dell's most ambitious series to date—THE MORLAND DYNASTY.

From the Wars of the Roses and Tudor England to
World War II, THE MORLAND DYNASTY traces the
lives, loves and fortunes of a great English family.

A DELL BOOK $3.50   #12677-0

Danielle Steel
SUMMER'S END

author of *The Promise*
and *Season of Passion*

As the wife of handsome, successful, inter-
national lawyer Marc Edouard Duras, Deanna
had a beautiful home, diamonds and elegant
dinners. But her husband was traveling between the glamorous capitals of the business
world, and all summer Deanna would be alone.
Until Ben Thomas found her—and laughter
and love took them both by surprise.

A Dell Book $3.50

The unforgettable saga of a
magnificent family

IN JOY AND IN SORROW

by

JOAN JOSEPH

They were the wealthiest Jewish family in Portugal, masters of
Europe's largest shipping empire. Forced to flee the scourge of
the Inquisition that reduced their proud heritage to ashes, they
crossed the ocean in a perilous voyage. Led by a courageous,
beautiful woman, they would defy fate to seize a forbidden
dream of love.

A Dell Book   **$3.50**   **(14367-5)**

At your local bookstore or use this handy coupon for ordering:

DELL BOOKS   **IN JOY AND IN SORROW**   **$3.50**   **(14367-5)**
P.O. BOX 1000, PINE BROOK, N.J. 07058-1000

Please send me the books I have checked above. I am enclosing $_____ (please add 75c per copy to
cover postage and handling). Send check or money order—no cash or C.O.D.'s. Please allow up to 8 weeks for
shipment.

Mr./Mrs./Miss_____

Address_____

City_____State/Zip_____